"I shouldn't hav

Rhys forced himself to ~~be blunt, continuing,~~ complicates things. If we're not careful it could *change* things. Between us. I don't want that. It was a mistake.'

"Obviously it was," Mariah said in a voice kept determinedly colorless. She wouldn't let him see the pain his words caused. She should have known.

"So," Rhys said briskly after a moment. "Are we friends?"

"We're friends," she managed. "But things won't ever be quite the same."

He frowned. "Why not? You said—"

"I'm pregnant, Rhys. I'm going to have your child."

* * * * *

Rhys has two brothers, Nathan and Dominic.
Look out for future books by Anne McAllister
featuring these tantalising, tough,
untamed men!

Anne McAllister was born in California. She spent long lazy summers daydreaming on local beaches and studying surfers, swimmers and volleyball players in an effort to find the perfect hero. She finally did, not on the beach, but in a university library where she was working. She, her husband and their four children have since moved to the Midwest. She taught, copy-edited, capped deodorant bottles, and ghostwrote sermons before turning to her first love, writing romance fiction.

Recent titles by the same author:

GIBSON'S GIRL

RHYS'S
REDEMPTION

BY
ANNE McALLISTER

MILLS & BOON®

MILLS & BOON and MILLS & BOON with the Rose Device are registered trademarks of the publisher.

First published in Great Britain 2000
Harlequin Mills & Boon Limited,
Eton House, 18-24 Paradise Road, Richmond, Surrey TW9 1SR

© Barbara Schenck 2000

ISBN 0 263 82022 X

Set in Times Roman 10½ on 11½ pt.
01-0010-46800

Printed and bound in Spain
by Litografía Rosés, S.A., Barcelona

CHAPTER ONE

RHYS WOLFE wanted a hot shower, a cold beer, and twenty-four hours of sleep—in that order.

It was six a.m. in New York City, buses were rumbling, horns were honking, the city was waking up. And he was ready to hit the sack.

It wasn't six a.m. in his head. He wasn't sure, in fact, what time it was. All he knew was that he'd been playing "planes, trains and automobiles" for hours, and he was ready to drop.

He fumbled with his key in the lock to the ornate steel gate under the stoop that led to his brownstone garden apartment, glancing warily up at the flat two floors above as he did so.

Was Mariah up?

Lying in wait?

Yeah. Sure. Like she'd been standing at the window for the past nine weeks just waiting to catch a glimpse of him.

Like she cared.

Rhys twisted the key, opened the gate, then the door to his apartment. That was the trouble. She *did* care.

Mariah was his friend. And he was hers.

Or had been.

He didn't know what he was now.

He shut the door behind him, dropped his duffel bag on the floor, shut his eyes and sagged against the door, letting the weariness—and the worry—overtake him.

He hadn't been home in over two months. Not since...

Not since he'd awakened to find himself in bed with his upstairs neighbor.

His delectable, delightful upstairs neighbor. His friend. Mariah.

God, what a mess. Usually he was eager to get home, looking forward to a respite from the demands and stress of his job as part of a specialized firefighting unit. Usually he could hardly wait to give Mariah a call and see what she'd been up to for the past few weeks.

He sighed and rolled his shoulders, then began unbuttoning his shirt. Now he didn't want to call her at all. He didn't know what to say to her.

That was the trouble, he thought, with having sex with a woman you cared about. It complicated things. Messed everything up. Led to unreasonable expectations.

Like a relationship.

Like marriage.

No. Rhys shook his head fiercely as he shed his shirt and headed toward the bathroom. Mariah knew better than that.

She, of all people, knew how he felt about marriage. She'd heard him expound on the subject often enough.

Rhys Wolfe wasn't looking for marriage, for commitment, for responsibility. He'd been there, done that. He wasn't doing it again.

And he made it a point to say that to every woman he met who might be tempted to think otherwise. It was a precaution. Good common sense. That way none of them could say she hadn't been warned.

The only women who went to bed with Rhys Wolfe knew the score. Having sex with Rhys meant fun and games. No strings attached.

Rhys never slept with women to whom it might mean more than that.

It was his first rule of self-preservation—a rule he'd made eight years ago. And he'd never broken it.

Until that night nine weeks back.

Right after Jack died.

Jack.

He'd just finished the first assignment he'd done without Jack. Tough, competent, laughing Jack. The one they'd always marveled at—the man death couldn't touch.

"Lucky Jack," his friends, the guys on his high-intensity, high-risk, internationally known oil well and rig firefighting team, always called him.

"I'll go with Jack," they always said when the danger in their job was greater than usual. "Jack's lucky."

But ten weeks ago, on a North Sea rig, Jack's luck had run out. It had happened during a fire no different than those they'd fought a hundred times before. No one had been careless. No one had screwed up. As hard as he tried, Rhys still couldn't nail down a reason for what happened.

Other than that Jack's time had been up.

Lucky Jack's luck had run out.

Five days later Rhys had come home from his best friend's funeral, still reeling, shattered, angry and distraught. Mourning Jack had been bad enough, but worse than that even had been the memories that had crowded his mind.

Memories of another fire, another funeral—Sarah's—eight years before.

Sarah. His wife.

Sarah, his childhood love.

Sarah's time hadn't been up! Rhys was sure of it. She hadn't had to die.

If he'd been home that night instead of working ridiculously long hours, if he'd been with her, like a proper husband, instead of trying, and failing, to be the perfect son, Sarah—and their unborn child—would be alive today.

But he hadn't been.

He'd been in the family business then—right out of college and determined to prove himself, to show his father and his oldest brother, Dominic, that he could work as many hours as they could, be as successful as they were. He hadn't even gone home for dinner. He'd worked right through, stopping only to call Sarah and say, "I'll be late. Don't wait up."

She hadn't. Under doctor's orders to get lots of rest, Sarah had gone to bed early that night. But first, apparently, she'd lit a candle. At least that was what the fire marshal told him later.

"I'll leave a light on for you," she'd told Rhys.

A candle.

She'd been asleep when the fire broke out in their apartment. She'd never awakened.

He'd lost her—and their child—that night.

And nothing Rhys could do would bring them back.

He understood that. Eventually he'd managed to accept it.

He lived with the pain. And the guilt.

To his father's consternation, Rhys had quit his job with the family firm, choosing instead to go into firefighting.

"What the hell for?" his dad had demanded. "It isn't going to bring Sarah back."

"No." Rhys knew that. But he needed to do it. Needed to battle again and again the demons that took his wife from him. To do what he could to win the fight he'd lost before he knew how much it mattered.

He was a good firefighter. Determined. Focussed. Cool and controlled in the face of the flames.

And so he atoned. Or tried to.

Over the past eight years, he'd got past it. He was sure of that. He had a life now. A new apartment on the West Side, away from the East Side neighborhood where he and Sarah had lived. He had friends. And, now and then, he had women.

But he wasn't marrying again. Ever.

He wasn't letting himself get close to anyone again. That

part he hadn't got past. Loving someone the way he'd loved Sarah hurt too much.

He couldn't do it again.

Wouldn't. Ever.

So he always kept things light. He had friends. He had the occasional lover. But never a friend who was also a lover.

Until he came home after Jack had died. That night the grief and the memories had swallowed him whole.

And Mariah—poor unsuspecting Mariah—surprised to see his light on, had stopped by to tap on his door and see what was going on.

He didn't remember much of what happened after that.

He'd tried not to. For over two months he had tried not to.

He hadn't wanted to remember how she'd held him in her arms, had kissed him and soothed him, had let him—a man who needed no one—cling to her like a child.

He shut that out.

Just as he shut out how, in another way, he'd felt very much unlike a child. The flames of need had licked at him, had driven him to kiss her, to touch her, to seek the softness of her. His body had needed the solace of her. Desperately.

And slowly, gently, and then with what his shattered mind remembered as a passion equal to his, Mariah had given it to him.

He gritted his teeth. He couldn't think about that.

Couldn't let himself remember.

Because when he did, even now, his body betrayed him, and he wanted it to happen again.

It couldn't happen again!

He wouldn't let it.

He cared about Mariah. As a friend. He wouldn't let it become more.

He could still remember how shocked he'd been to awaken and find her asleep beside him in his bed.

Rhys had never *slept* with any woman—not since Sarah. It was too intimate. It implied too much.

But that night he had slept with Mariah. When he'd finally opened his eyes in the pale dawn, it was to find her curled around him, her cheek nestled against his shoulder, a leg casually draped over his, one arm across his belly and tucked against his hip.

He'd been afraid to breathe. He hadn't dared move.

But he'd needed to. Desperately. He knew he had to get out of there—without awakening her.

What the hell would he have said to her if he'd still been there when she opened her eyes?

He hadn't known then.

He didn't know now.

He'd spent the past nine weeks trying to figure it out.

He was still hoping something would occur to him when he saw her. Maybe, with luck—and knowing how he felt about that sort of thing—Mariah would take the lead. Maybe she would make light of it, blow it off. Maybe she would tell him it didn't matter, would let him off the hook.

He drew a shaky breath. Yes, she could do that. She was that kind of woman. Generous. Kind. Rhys liked her enormously.

One of the things he liked best about her was that she was nothing like Sarah.

Mariah was tall and slender. Willowy, he sometimes thought, but resilient. Strong. She wasn't fragile or petite like Sarah had been. She embraced the world with open arms. Sarah had always been more cautious, content to let him take the lead.

Their hair was different, too. Sarah had had a blonde pixie cut that he could ruffle with his fingers. Mariah had long brown hair, the color of chestnuts, that he remembered tangling his fingers in that night.

He gave his head a shake and shoved the memory away.

He needed to think about Mariah as a friend. He needed to get things back on that footing. It was what they both wanted after all. She'd never done anything to make him believe she wanted more. It was what had made him comfortable with her in the first place.

She'd always just been his friend.

From the first time he'd met her, when she was having a cookout on her terrace and had invited all the neighbors, she'd made him feel like a good friend. Always cheerful and easy to talk to, Mariah was the perfect neighbor. She was fun—to do things with, to talk to. He loved going jogging with her or to a film or a new restaurant or a gallery opening with her when he was home.

And she never demanded more.

He didn't want to lose that.

She wouldn't want to lose it either. He hoped. He ran a hand through his uncombed hair and yawned.

After he'd showered and slept, he decided, then he would face her. He would tell her how much he valued her friendship, how he didn't want to ruin it, how he wanted things to be the way they had been before.

And then he would grin at her and say, "Want to go to the top of the Empire State Building?"

And she would know that everything was the same.

It had started as a joke between them three years ago when Mariah found out that she, a transplant from Kansas, had been up to the top of the Empire State Building and that Rhys, a native New Yorker, never had.

She had insisted he had to go. He'd put her off. Once. Twice. A dozen times at least.

Until finally she'd grabbed him as they'd been walking

home from a film late one night. She'd hailed a cab and directed the driver to Thirty-fourth Street.

"Don't be crazy," he'd protested.

But over Rhys's groans she'd insisted. "It's beautiful. Magical," she'd told him. "You have to see it."

She was right. It had been magical. They'd gone late enough that there weren't very many people there. It had been a beautiful clear night and New York had been spread out below them, glittering like a fistful of diamonds tossed by a giant.

It was breathtaking. Rhys couldn't believe he'd ignored it for so many years.

"See?" Mariah had said, watching him, not the view.

"I see," he'd said. And in fact he'd been the one to insist they stay, just walking around looking, until at last they were thrown out.

They'd gone back many times after that. Almost every time he'd come home they'd gone.

Except the last time.

Rhys drew a harsh breath again as he remembered what they'd done the last time. Then once more he tried to shove the thought away.

It didn't matter. It was over.

This time they'd go.

He started toward the shower and was tempted by the refrigerator's hum as he passed the kitchen. Visions of that nice cold bottle of beer swirled through his sleep-deprived head. But he knew from experience that the beer would taste a whole lot better when he was clean.

He had a month's worth of Middle Eastern sand, dust and grit to scrub off this time, not to mention the oil and grime and ash residue from the fire.

It wasn't that he hadn't showered. It was that it never did any good.

There was always more dust, more sand, more ash, more

grime. It got, almost literally, under his skin. And he knew from experience that as long as he was there—wherever *there* was this time—he wasn't going to be rid of it until he got home again.

He kicked off his shoes and socks and stripped off his khakis and shorts as he went down the hall, letting them lie where they fell. He was naked by the time he padded into the bathroom and turned on the shower.

In seconds he had a cascade of hot water. It was bliss.

As far as Rhys was concerned, the best thing about his apartment was the hot water heater. He didn't mind cold, short serviceable showers at work, but when he came home he wanted hot water and lots of it.

In fact, he needed it. He knew from experience that it would take gallons and gallons to get rid of the remaining physical vestiges of the fire he'd battled last.

It would take longer yet for the memory of the flames to recede and for the everyday life everyone else took for granted to nudge its way past the curtain of smoke and fire that separated his work from their lives.

He took his time, letting the water wash over him. He welcomed the beat of it on his skull. It felt clean, pure, fresh.

He felt better. More alive. He began to whistle as he soaped his lean, hard body quickly. Then with rough, cal-lused fingers he scrubbed the shampoo into his scalp, then ducked his head once more and rinsed it out again.

A glance showed him that the water running off looked clean enough now. So he shut off the taps, grabbed a towel and began to dry himself.

Then he brushed his teeth and ran a hand over his heavily whiskered jaw. He hadn't shaved in five days at least—hadn't had time. Now he decided it could wait another twelve hours.

He scrubbed the towel once more over his head, getting

most of the dampness out of his short dark hair. Then he padded, still naked, face in the towel as he rubbed his scalp, toward the bedroom—and bumped into something soft yet undeniably firm.

"What the—?" He jerked back, lowered the towel, and felt a shock jolt right through him. He gaped. *"Mariah?"*

The last person he expected to see—the very last person he *wanted* to see—was standing in the doorway to *his* bedroom wearing a skimpy pale blue cotton nightgown—and not much else. Her dark hair was sleep-tousled and tangled, her face was pale and as shocked as his as she stared at him. In her arms she clutched a pile of clothes.

"What the hell are you doing here?" he demanded.

Mariah would have liked to ask him the same thing!

Odd sounds had awakened her from a sound sleep. At first she'd fitted them into her dream. Footsteps. Water running. But then there was the whistling.

She couldn't fit in whistling.

And that was when she'd woken up. She'd lain there for long moments trying to sort things out. And then, with a shaft of clear thought and blinding panic, she'd realized the only thing it could be: Rhys!

She'd scrambled out of bed, grabbed her clothes and headed for the door. She'd get dressed in her own apartment. Get herself put together. And then she'd come back to face him.

Instead she ran smack into him coming out of the bathroom.

And all he was wearing was a towel—over his head!

Then he lowered it. They stared at each other in astonishment. And rapidly, thank God, he shifted the towel south.

Mariah swallowed hastily. "I'm sorry. I didn't mean to surprise you. I was… You always told me I could use your place when you were gone…if I had guests." She was making a hash of it. Damn him for surprising her! "My cousin Erica is here with her family…from Emporia. I thought it would be easier to let them have my place." *And I didn't have a clue you'd be back!*

He rubbed a hand down his face, then smiled at her. "Hey, it doesn't matter," he said cheerfully. "I remember what I told you. Of course it's okay." He gave a wave of his hand. "No problem. Go back to bed. I'll crash on the sofa."

"No." She didn't want that. She wanted to talk to him. To clear the air. But not now. Not like this. "Don't be ridiculous. You're obviously exhausted. You'll have your bed. It's time for me to get up anyway. I'll just change these sheets and be out of your way." She turned away as she spoke and hurried back into his room to rip the sheets off the bed.

She could feel Rhys's gaze on her even as she worked. She wished she'd taken the time to brush past him and into the bathroom where she could dress. She knew her nightgown was barely covering her rear end. And she knew he knew it, too.

Still, she wasn't sure he'd care.

He might have made love with her last time he was home, but Mariah wasn't fool enough to think it had meant anything to him. Even if she wished it had!

She ripped the sheets off the bed quickly and efficiently, not even glancing his way. Then she was aware of him edging around her, and realized that he was trying to get to his dresser to get some clothes.

"Sorry," she muttered, face flaming. "I'll get out of your way."

She tried to. And he grabbed his stuff and yanked it on. Mariah tried not to notice him out of the corner of her eye. But it was difficult. He had a beautiful body—hard and lean and muscular. His chest was lightly dusted with dark hair that arrowed down toward his groin and—

She let out a harsh breath and reached for a clean sheet with trembling hands.

"I can do that," Rhys said. "Really. It's okay. And it's fine that you stayed here. It's what I gave you a key for, remember? Because we're friends."

Yes, they were friends. Or they had been.

She didn't know what they would be now.

"I wouldn't have stayed," she told him, bending to tuck in the sheet, "if I'd known."

"Why not?"

She wished he wouldn't press the issue right now. She wanted to be calm, together, in control. But he was. She sighed and flung open a sheet. "You know why not."

"Because of what happened," Rhys said flatly.

For a second the only thing moving was the sheet as it fluttered into place on the bed. Then Mariah nodded her head.

"We have to talk about that."

No kidding. "Yes, we do. I know how you feel about—"

"Right," he said quickly. "And you do, too. Don't you? Why ruin a good thing, right? So we just go on from here."

She blinked. "Huh?"

He shrugged. "It was a one-off. A fluke. It just…happened. It doesn't have to change anything."

Mariah stared at him. She felt a wave of nausea begin to overtake her. Her skin felt cold and suddenly clammy. She thought the color must have drained from her face and was angry that it had. After all, this was what she'd expected.

"It doesn't," he insisted. "We were friends. *Are friends,*" he corrected himself. "And what we…what we did…that night, it doesn't have to wreck that."

"No, but—"

"It won't," he insisted. "We won't do it again. Look, Mariah," he said and she thought his tone was almost gentle now. "I know you were being kind when you... When you thought I needed..."

He stopped. She saw him swallow. She saw, too, that he wouldn't say the words. He wouldn't admit that he *had* needed.

Now he ran his tongue over his lips and took a steadying breath. "It was a hard time for me. The funeral. Jack dying like that."

But it wasn't only Jack, Mariah knew that. Jack had been the catalyst. But the need had gone deeper. It had gone back to Sarah, the wife he wouldn't talk about unless he'd had too many beers and was too far gone to remember to keep his mouth shut.

Sarah, the only woman he'd ever loved.

Mariah held herself very still.

Rhys took a breath. "You were being kind and...I shouldn't have...shouldn't have done...what I did. I was...out of my head. I took advantage. I broke my rule."

"What rule?"

"About sex. About not having sex with friends. You know that. I don't have sex with friends."

"You have sex with your enemies?"

A harsh breath hissed through his teeth. "No. Of course not! But I don't have sex with women I care about, either! Not...not like that."

"Like what?"

Rhys raked a hand through his hair. She saw the exhaustion in him, the confusion, and she knew she shouldn't press him. This wasn't the time.

But it had gone too far, and he was going to finish. "I shouldn't have slept with you. Had sex with you." He forced himself to be blunt. "It complicates things. If we're not careful it could *change* things. Between us. I don't want that. It was a mistake.''

So, there it was. She'd asked for it.

Their lovemaking had been, in Rhys's eyes, a mistake.

"Obviously it was," she said in a voice kept determinedly colorless. She wouldn't let him see the pain his words caused. She should have known.

Damn it, she *had* known! But that night she couldn't help herself.

Rhys smiled. He held out a hand. "So," he said briskly after a moment, "no hard feelings?"

She didn't answer. She didn't take his hand either. She looked at him and then away. She tried to regroup. To become the person he wanted her to become.

His friend.

His buddy.

His pal.

When she didn't take his hand, he dropped it to his side. But he couldn't let it rest. "Mariah?" He smiled hopefully, encouragingly, once more. "Are we friends?"

She gathered up her clothes and the sheets, then clutched them against her heart as if they were a shield. Then she dipped her head. "We're friends," she managed.

He grinned. He let out a whoosh of relief. "Great."

She brushed past him, headed down the hall, still cold, still clammy, more nauseated than ever. At the end of the hall she turned back. "But things won't ever be quite the same," she told him.

He frowned. "Why not? You said—"

"I'm pregnant, Rhys. I'm going to have your child."

CHAPTER TWO

MARIAH hadn't expected him to be thrilled.

She, better than anyone, knew Rhys's attitude about family.

"Not interested," he'd said bluntly the first time they'd discussed it when they'd known each other only a few months. She'd asked him to go with her to her friend Lizzie's wedding and he'd gone willingly enough. They'd been at the reception when the topic of marriage had come up, and just as quickly Rhys had put it back down again.

"I've been married. Never again," he'd said adamantly.

At the time she didn't know about his background, and she remembered staring at him, astonished at his vehemence. While most guys she knew carefully shied away from the matrimonial lasso, they'd seemed merely skittish, not fierce in their determination.

Not Rhys.

"So if you meet the right girl, you'll just tell her to get lost?" She'd teased him a little for his uncompromising stance, expecting he'd relent a little.

But Rhys had said flatly, "It will never get that far. There will never be another right girl. I won't let it happen."

So she'd been warned. She couldn't say she hadn't been.

But, warned or not, it hadn't made any difference. She'd fallen in love with him anyway.

She'd known him for three years, ever since she'd bought the flat above his in the brownstone co-op where they lived. She'd lived by him, talked with him, eaten with him, laughed with him, played with him. Discovered that he was everything she'd ever wanted in a man.

And he never knew.

Because by the time she'd been aware of it herself she knew he wasn't looking for a relationship.

He didn't want another love.

And so she'd never asked for more than he would give. For three years she had been what he wanted her to be: his friend. His buddy. The one he called to go jogging or to toss a Frisbee around in the park. The one he called to say, "How about catching that Brazilian film tonight at Lincoln Plaza?" The one he nursed a beer with at McCabe's, the neighborhood bar. The one he tried out the newest trendy restaurant with, or went to the latest museum exhibit, or to a Yankees game, or to the Cloisters with.

She was the only person he'd ever been to the Empire State Building with. Though once he'd thought maybe they should take Jack.

Now they never would.

Now they might never go there again together—because Mariah had seen the shock on Rhys's face. She'd seen the swift denial in his eyes. She'd seen the mixture of fury and pain flichering in them.

Any hopes she might have had that, faced with the reality of her pregnancy, he'd change his mind about things died right then.

But reality was still the same.

In seven months Mariah was going to have Rhys Wolfe's baby—whether he liked it or not, whether he wanted it or not.

She wanted it.

Now that she'd had time to come to terms with it, Mariah very definitely wanted it.

Not that getting pregnant had been her intention when she'd gone down to Rhys's apartment that evening nine weeks ago.

She'd gone out of curiosity—and concern.

She knew as well as anyone that Rhys's schedule was never cut in stone. As a member of an elite firefighting unit, one called in wherever oil rig, well or refinery fires got out of hand, he never knew when he might be taking off for a distant spot on the globe.

He never cared.

"What do I have to stay home for?" he'd once said with a shrug. "I like what I do."

Besides the actual firefighting, he spent a fair amount of time teaching firefighting skills in clinics worldwide. Those were a little more predictable. But Mariah never knew exactly when he would be back until she heard a rap on her door and found Rhys standing there with a heart-stopping grin on his face, saying, "You wanta go up the Empire State Building, lady?"

That night, when she'd seen his light on, she'd been surprised as he'd only left less than a week before to go to England. It was unusual for him to be back so soon. She'd been afraid something might be wrong.

So she'd gone down and knocked on his door. When he hadn't answered, she'd let herself in with the key he'd given her so she could keep an eye on things.

She'd called his name. He hadn't replied.

She knew which light he'd rigged to turn on when he was gone. But it wasn't the one she'd seen from her terrace, the one in his bedroom, which opened onto the small back garden.

So she'd called his name again. "Rhys? Are you home?"

Then she'd spotted his duffel bag next to the desk, and for just a moment she felt happiness quicken her heart as it always did when she knew he was home.

Because she was always glad to see him.

And if there was more to it than that on her part, she deliberately tried never to think about it because she didn't want to ruin what they had by asking for more than he could give. What she had, she was determined, would be enough.

When she'd gone down the hall, she'd found the door of his bedroom open and the lamp by his bed spilling light across the polished oak floor. "Rhys?"

She'd stopped at the door, then peered in. The sliding door that led into the garden was open, too, and the vertical blinds rattled lightly in the late-night breeze.

She smiled, sure she would find him outside looking up at the stars, drinking in the relative quiet of the city at nearly midnight. They'd sat back here many times late into the night, talking about everything under the moon. He liked to do that. He said it helped him unwind.

Perhaps, if he wasn't too tired, they would do that tonight. So she didn't hesitate to join him.

He was there, as she'd thought, sitting in one of the Adirondack chairs, his head thrown back, eyes shut. His lean cheeks seemed almost hollow in the moonlight, his firm mouth tight. His arms lay limply on the armrests. An almost empty glass sat beside his hand. On the ground, next to the chair, there was a whiskey bottle.

Mariah's brows lifted in surprise. Rhys rarely drank hard liquor. He liked a cold beer on a warm day, but that was all.

"Rhys?"

He didn't move, and she thought he might have fallen asleep. Then his jaw tightened further. He swallowed. She saw his Adam's apple move in his throat. His fingers gripped the arms of the chair, and slowly he opened his eyes and turned his head her way.

There wasn't enough light from the bedroom for her to see his expression. But she could see the way he moved.

Like an old man.

She hurried toward him.

"Rhys?" She knew something wasn't right. She didn't see exhaustion. She saw pain. She knelt beside him, taking his hand in hers. It was icy as it clenched hers. "What happened? What's wrong?"

He didn't speak. He just stared. And then he said, "Jack."

It was like a blow. She knew at once.

She'd met Jack O'Day several times. She'd been charmed by his dark good looks, his unfailing good cheer, his Irish wit and casual grace. He had none of Rhys's dark, brooding intensity, none of his fierce determination. Jack was the embodiment of hail-fellow-well-met. The opposite of Rhys.

They were, in Jack's words, "O'Day and O'Night."

But, for all their differences, they were closer than brothers. Two halves of a whole, Mariah had thought. Complementary souls.

Best friends. Had been since their rookie days on the team.

And, seeing the stark pain on Rhys's face, she knew. He didn't need to say more.

She reached out and put her arms around him, drew him close, held him tight.

And without a word Rhys wrapped his arms around her. He clung to her like a drowning man, pressing his face into the curve of her neck. Silent tears scalded her, and she felt the tremble of his hard body against her own.

She didn't know how long she held him there, didn't know when they rose and moved from the garden into the house. She didn't know when their embrace ceased to be comfort and became something more, when the feelings became something stronger, and when Rhys's need became desperate and something that only she could give.

Maybe she should have stopped it.

She, of the two, had a better chance at control, at calling a halt, holding him off, saying no.

Or maybe she didn't.

Maybe, if she was honest, she never had. Not for months. Or years.

Because that was how long she'd loved him.

So she didn't say no when his lips found hers. She didn't say no when he ran his hands up under her shirt, when he peeled off her shorts and stripped off his jeans, when they fell onto the bed in each other's arms, and found solace in each other's bodies.

She didn't *want* to say no.

She wanted the night. The love. The sharing.

She wanted Rhys.

She had hoped—had spent the last nine weeks hoping— that their one night of loving would become something more. Something deeper. Something lasting.

She hadn't intended the lasting part to be his child.

Of course, she should have taken precautions. But what had happened hadn't been premeditated.

Making love with Rhys Wolfe had been the last thing on her mind. When it happened, it had surprised her as much as it had him. But she wasn't sorry.

And maybe she should be, she thought now as, still clutching his sheets and her clothes, she made her way slowly up the steps to her own apartment.

But she wasn't.

She had regrets, yes.

But not for their lovemaking—and not for the child they'd made.

What she regretted was that Rhys still thought it was a mistake.

She didn't know how to change his mind. She only knew she had to.

And she would. Later.

Right now she had to make it back to her apartment before morning sickness overtook her.

"What do you mean you're going to—?" Rhys stopped dead and glared at the brown-haired young woman who had just opened Mariah's apartment door. *"Who the hell are you?"*

"I'm Erica, Mariah's cousin." The brunette blinked nervously at his vehemence, then managed a smile. "And you must be Rhys."

"Why?"

Did she know? he wondered. Had Mariah told everyone before him?

Erica swallowed rapidly, nervously. "I just…guessed. When she came back just now, Mariah said you were home. I hope you don't mind that she was using your apartment while we were here. She said you wouldn't, but…" The look she was giving him said she didn't necessarily believe that. But she didn't look at him as if she knew anything about him and Mariah and a child.

Rhys breathed marginally easier. "I didn't mind if she uses my apartment," he said curtly. "Now where is she?"

He'd followed her upstairs the minute he'd got his wits together. He still wasn't sure he'd heard her right. He couldn't have heard her right! She hadn't said she was pregnant.

Had she?

"She's in the bathroom. Taking a shower, I think."

Rhys's fists clenched. Hiding out, he translated. He ground his teeth, then brushed past the cousin and stalked into the living room. "I'll wait."

He wanted to throttle her. How could she say something like that, then just bolt up the stairs, leaving him standing there, pole-axed? He still couldn't fathom it. Pregnant?

With *his* child?

He glowered around now, trying to fix on something to vent his frustration. Something to shatter or smash or strangle. There was nothing.

Not even Mariah's apartment looked familiar. Her normally neat, albeit comfortably homey living room was messy and cluttered. It looked as if it had been taken over by aliens. With children.

There were toys scattered on the floor and clothes piled on the chairs. There was nowhere to sit. The sofa had been pulled out to make a bed and a little boy in pajamas was sprawled on it, staring at a cartoon on the television. He glanced at Rhys with minimal interest, then went back to the animated violence.

Somebody was bopping a rabbit over the head with a mallet. The rabbit's head was spinning. Stars wheeled around his ears. He had a stupefied look on his face.

He looked the way Rhys felt.

Mariah was *pregnant*?

Every time he put those three words in that order, it was like taking a blow to the gut.

"Tyler, sit up and let Mr....er...Rhys...sit down. That's Tyler," she said to Rhys. "My son. Can I get you some coffee while you wait? Mariah said you'd be going to sleep now, so I don't know if you'd want any coffee, but..."

Going to sleep?

Mariah had told him she was going to have his baby, walked out, and expected he would *go to sleep*?

Not bloody likely.

"No coffee," he said brusquely. His nerves were already shot. He prowled, he paced.

A sudden infantile wail sounded in the bedroom.

Rhys jumped. "What the hell was *that*?"

"Oh, that's just Ashley," Erica said cheerfully. "Our daughter. Jeff—my husband—is changing her. He had to come to New York for a seminar this week, so we came with him." As she spoke she poured two mugs of coffee and handed one to Rhys just as if he hadn't already declined.

Maybe he looked like he needed fortification. God knew he felt as if he did. He clutched the mug in his hands like a lifeline.

"Mariah is Ty's godmother," Erica went on, "and it's been ages since she's seen him and she'd *never* seen Ashley. So we decided we'd all come and visit. Mariah and Sierra don't get home often and we miss them a lot. You know how it is with families," she said brightly.

"No," he said. "I don't."

Erica blinked.

Rhys wished to hell Mariah would get out here. How could she do this to him? He rocked on his heels. He ground his teeth. His fingers clenched on the coffee mug as if he were strangling it.

"You don't have any family?" Erica sounded as if she pitied him.

Rhys scowled. He didn't want anybody's pity. "I have brothers," he said curtly.

"Oh, well, that's good." She smiled brightly. "And did you grow up in the city?"

Rhys raked a hand through his hair. Again he paced from one end of the room to the other, avoiding the piles of clothes and toys and pillows. He did not want to make polite conversation with this woman while Mariah hid out in the bathroom!

Finally he slapped the mug down on the counter with such force that the coffee spilled. "I've got to go. Tell her I need to talk to her," he bit out. "Tell her to come down."

Mariah wasn't at all sure she wanted to hear anything Rhys had to say. She'd hoped that a shower and a handful of soda crackers would have equipped her for dealing with him.

She was afraid she was out of luck. She concentrated on braiding her hair.

"He came looking for you," Erica said, her voice dripping curiosity. "He really wanted you."

Mariah could hear the double entendre in her cousin's voice. Would that it were true, she thought. "I'll go see him later," she said. When she felt steadier on her feet, stronger. More capable.

"He's a hunk," Erica said. "Why haven't you told us about him before?"

"Nothing to tell," Mariah said airily.

"He seems interested."

"Not...like that."

"Too bad," Erica said. "Is he gay?"

Mariah almost choked. "What?"

"Well, if he isn't, why isn't he interested? You're single, smart, gorgeous, in possession of all your teeth. What more could he want?"

"He doesn't even want that much," Mariah said.

Erica leaned closer. Mariah could see her cousin's freckles in the mirror. "What?"

She shook her head. "Never mind." She finished braiding her hair and straightened her shoulders. She felt marginally better. Not as if she was going to puke anymore. That was one of the reasons she'd stayed down at Rhys's—so she wouldn't be up here puking every morning and giving Erica lots more to speculate about.

She hadn't told anyone she was pregnant yet. She'd been waiting to tell Rhys first.

And now? she asked herself. Now that she'd told him...

She still couldn't bring herself to tell Erica. She would have to answer too many questions. Or she wouldn't—and she would be subject to way too much scrutiny because of that.

In either case, it wasn't something she was ready to talk about. Not now.

Not yet.

If Rhys had been happy about it...if he'd grinned and whooped and swung her up in his arms the way Mariah's friend Chloe's husband, Gibson, had when she'd told him she was expecting their child...well, then Mariah would have been happy to share the news with the world.

But Rhys hadn't.

He'd looked stricken. Aghast.

Her jaw tightened. She sucked in a careful breath. *Oh, Rhys!*

"Go talk to him," Erica said. "Ask him if he wants to come with us to the Empire State Building."

Mariah nearly snorted. She could just imagine what Rhys would say to that!

"He's the one you go with all the time, isn't he?" Erica persisted.

"Yes."

"So he'd probably like to go."

"He just got home."

"You can ask."

"All right," Mariah said. "I'll ask."

"Ask what?" Jeff, Erica's husband, came into the room carrying eight-month-old Ashley. He handed the baby to his wife, then dropped a kiss on her mouth. The way they looked at each other was so full of love that Mariah was torn between watching in unabashed envy and turning away for the very same reason.

She wanted a love like that.

"Ask Mariah's hunky friend to come with us today," Erica said.

"Mariah has a hunky friend?" Jeff's eyebrows lifted.

"He's a friend," Mariah said firmly.

"And a hunk," Erica chimed in. "I know you don't *need* a man, Mariah," she said quickly. "But they are nice to have around."

Mariah didn't have to be told that. She wasn't quite sure where the family had got the notion that she couldn't be bothered. Maybe it was because she was thirty-one years old and for the past eight years she had been working her butt off to become a successful journalist for a lifestyle magazine with national circulation, which didn't leave a lot of time for finding the perfect man.

But that didn't mean she wasn't interested.

She was. Very.

She might have a boss who thought she was fantastic and colleagues who admired her. The subjects of her articles, many of whom had been burned by the press before, might have nothing but good things to say about her. Mariah Kelly might be one of the most respected and sought-after chroniclers of the rich and famous in America today, a woman who was successful beyond the wildest dreams of the studious, determined small-town girl she had once been.

But that didn't mean her life was perfect the way it was.

It didn't mean she wanted to spend the rest of it without a man.

One man.

The man. The one she loved.

Rhys.

She sucked in a careful breath. She couldn't put it off forever. She would have to talk to him—and listen to him—sometime.

Please, God, she said in the silence of her heart, *I love him. Make this work.*

He couldn't figure out what to do with his hands.

He jammed them in his pockets. He balled them into

fists. He cracked his knuckles one after another. He raked his fingers through his hair. He stuffed them into his pockets again and turned to glare at her.

How the hell could she just sit there on the sofa so calmly while he paced and muttered and tried to fix the mess that had suddenly become his life?

"I told you how I feel about family." He knew the words sounded accusing. He couldn't help it. He was doing his best to not to let the strain show in his voice. Rhys was noted for his calm under pressure—just ask anyone he worked with. He felt as if the top of his head was going to come off now!

Mariah nodded. "I know how you feel about family. What you said, that is. And I...understand. But—"

"Then how could you—?"

"It wasn't just me!" she retorted, not so calm now, her voice rising, too. "I didn't do this by myself, Rhys!"

He pounded one fist into the other hand. "Damn it! I know that! I just... Hell!" He shut his eyes and prayed for strength. He didn't find it. He said a harsh word. And then another.

When he opened his eyes again, he saw Mariah looking at him, stricken. As if he'd just stabbed her.

He supposed he had. But he'd been stabbed, too. Trapped. Nailed.

The one thing he'd set off-limits, the very last thing he ever wanted, was here, now, staring him in the face.

"I wasn't counting on this," he muttered what had to be the greatest understatement of his life.

"And you think I was?"

"No, of course not! I didn't say that. It must be just as bad for you as for—"

"No." She cut him off.

He stopped. And stared. "What?"

"I said, no." And she shook her head to make the point. "It isn't bad. It isn't," she repeated. "I admit I was shocked when I found out. Stunned, even. And dismayed—because it wasn't the way I'd thought about becoming pregnant." She smiled a little wistfully. "But I'm over that. I'm fine. I want this baby." She sounded absolutely resolute about that.

"You want it?" Pardon him if he sounded incredulous. "You're a career woman. You have a job!"

"Lots of women have jobs. And children. So will I."

"You never said you wanted kids!"

"You never asked," she replied.

He gaped at her. Then he shook his head, disbelieving. "It doesn't make sense. None of this makes sense." He gave her a hard, narrow look, wondering if he'd ever known her at all. She'd *never,* in the three years he'd known her, given the slightest indication that she was interested in marriage and family. That was why he'd liked her so damn much!

Well, that and because she was fun to be with, a good conversationalist, an intent listener and a compassionate, loving person.

He felt duped. Tricked.

"Did you…?" But he couldn't quite bring himself to voice the accusation.

She heard it anyway. Fire flashed in her normally gentle eyes. "No, I did not plan it! And if you even for one second think I did—" she wasn't calm at all now; she was seething "—you can go to hell!" She strode toward the door, chin high, back ramrod-straight.

He went after her, grabbing her arm and spinning her around. Suddenly they were bare inches apart, so close he could feel the heat of her breath against his cheek, so near that when her breasts heaved in indignation they nearly touched his chest.

And he remembered what it had been like when they had touched him. Remembered their softness, *her* softness.

He dropped her arm and stepped back, gathering his wits, striving for sanity. "I didn't think you had," he said heavily. "Not…really. I'm just…" he shoved his fingers through his hair again, spiking it into tufts "…I'm just…beat. It's…not something I was expecting."

She started to say something, but he held up his hand so she wouldn't interrupt. He needed to finish. "It's not that I didn't think about it…about what happened, I mean. I just never thought…about that."

Stupid as it was, he hadn't.

Maybe because all the women he'd had sex with since Sarah had died—and there hadn't been that many—had come "prepared." They'd known the score and had been looking for a good time as much as he had. They hadn't been looking for a family. Pregnancy had never been an option.

He looked at Mariah, but she wasn't looking at him. She was standing with her arms folded across her breasts, staring out the window toward the street. His eyes moved down in an almost reluctant attempt to discern any slight bulge. He couldn't see any, but he didn't remember Sarah showing at nine weeks either.

She'd only had the tiniest roundness when she'd…when she'd died.

His throat grew tight and ached. Something seemed to be throbbing at the back of his eyes. It hurt.

He hurt.

And at the same time he forced himself into a kind of detachment. A calm. The calm he'd managed after Sarah died, the sense of walking around in a glass bubble, disconnected from everything and everyone. Distant. Uninvolved.

It was the only way he could cope.

He took a breath, swallowed past the lump. He wet his lips. Then he said with quiet firmness, "I don't want to be married."

She flicked him a glance. "No one's asking you."

He blinked. Then, "You told me," he accused her.

She lifted her shoulders negligently. "Because you had a right to know. That's all. If you don't want anything to do with the baby—" she seemed to come down on the word with both feet "—or me, it's all right."

"It's damned well *not* all right! The whole thing is *not all right*! You're pregnant!" So much for calm and detachment.

"Yes. And I'm going to be a mother. I'm going to love being a mother." She shot him a defiant look, then her eyes softened. "But I'm not forcing you to be a father, Rhys."

He snorted bitterly. "According to you, that's already been accomplished."

"Only biologically."

That was enough. More than enough.

Rhys drew a shaky breath. His fingers tightened into fists as he steadied himself. "I'll give you money. I'll help financially. You won't want for a thing. The...baby—" he almost couldn't get his mouth around the word, but he did because he didn't want her to see how much it bothered him "—won't. But that's it. That's all I can do. All I will do. Understand?"

He expected an argument. He expected condemnation. He expected her to tell him what a selfish bastard he was.

He wouldn't deny it.

But she didn't argue and she didn't condemn. She just went to the door, then turned and met his gaze directly.

"Your choice, Rhys," she said quietly. "Your loss."

They went to the World Trade Center.

It was taller than the Empire State Building, Mariah told

them. If you were going to go up to the top of a skyscraper, she said and her voice didn't even waver, you might as well go for the tallest one around.

You could almost look right down on the Statue of Liberty from the World Trade Center, she explained. You could see Battery Park and get a view straight up the island of Manhattan from its southern tip. And afterwards you could go right on over to the Museum of the American Indian if you wanted to, or see Saint Paul's church or the Fraunces Tavern or spend the rest of the afternoon at South Street Seaport. She said it all with calm disinterest, as if she didn't really care which they chose.

"You don't have to convince us," Jeff said cheerfully. "We'll go wherever you tell us to go."

"The World Trade Center," Mariah decreed. *Not* the Empire State Building.

She couldn't have borne it.

If there had been Oscars for real-life acting, she deserved one. Not just for an afternoon of sightseeing when she wanted to crawl into a hole and die, but for having stayed composed while Rhys exploded, for not having shattered— well, not much—too.

But she'd managed it. It wouldn't have done any good to rant at him, to argue with him, to cajole. She would never cajole a man into wanting her—or their child. He had to want her because *he* wanted her—and the baby.

And she knew he would.

She hoped he would.

She prayed he would.

It would just take a little time.

She'd walked out dry-eyed and steady. And she'd gone right on being dry-eyed and steady all day long, even though Erica had bemoaned Rhys's not coming with them.

"He was too tired," Mariah explained.

And even though her cousin asked pointed questions about him the rest of the afternoon, she remained that way.

"He's a firefighter. He's gone a lot. I don't know," she said to the rest of the questions. "I don't know."

And eventually both Erica and Jeff became so enthralled with everything she showed them, and Tyler asked so many questions and was so busy darting here and there, and Ashley was busy demanding the attention that eight-month-old babies required, that no one noticed that sometimes Mariah's smile slipped and sometimes she knotted her fingers to stop them trembling, and that although the World Trade Center had a spectacular view up the length of Manhattan—"complete with the Empire State Building," Jeff said, "which is even better than going up in it"—in fact Mariah couldn't bring herself to look at it.

She stared at Staten Island instead.

And even then she didn't let herself remember the day she and Rhys had taken the ferry over there and back. She couldn't think about Rhys.

If she did, her emotions would go into overdrive. She would worry. She would fret. And she couldn't do anything about any of it.

It was hard to pay attention to the view.

"I'll keep an eye on Tyler," she told Erica and Jeff finally when they were torn between looking at the view or looking after their child. "Come on, buddy, let's give your mom and dad a break."

It was the best thing she could have done.

Tyler was a perfect distraction. He asked a thousand questions, not one of them about Rhys.

"How did they get that statue out there in the middle of that island?" he wanted to know, pointing at the Statue of Liberty. "Did a man carve it there? How do they build skyscrapers? Have they got basements? How do ferryboats run? Do they have rubber bands inside them like the ones

Daddy makes for me to use in the bathtub? How come that boat's got big tall sails? Why don't they make all buildings as big as this one? Why don't you live in a building this big, M'riah?''

He barely gave Mariah a chance to catch her breath between the answers. Just as well. She didn't want to think.

But she couldn't help it. She wondered if her child would be this inquisitive. Would it be eager and bouncy like Tyler or easygoing and placid like baby Ashley? Would it have her brown hair or the midnight-black of a man who said he didn't want a child at all?

She shoved that thought away.

She wondered what color eyes the baby would have. Her own soft dove-gray or the ice-chip blue of the man who had stared at her so fiercely this morning?

Her hand curved protectively against her abdomen as if she could shield her child from the anger and accusation in Rhys's hard gaze.

''You got a stomachache?'' Tyler asked.

Mariah made herself drop her hand and smile down at him. ''No,'' she said gently. ''I'm just getting hungry. I was thinking an ice-cream cone would be good right now. What do you say?''

Tyler grinned. ''Me, too!''

Rhys slept the clock around. And woke up feeling worse than when he'd gone to bed. For a moment he couldn't remember why.

Then he did.

It didn't seem real. Didn't seem possible.

He rolled over and groaned, then opened his eyes and recalled that the last time he'd slept here Mariah had been with him in the bed.

The memory was so vivid, so intense, so compelling that

even now his body hardened with desire. That wasn't supposed to happen!

He flung back the sheet and got out of bed.

He stumbled into the bathroom and turned on the cold water, then dunked his head under the tap. He scrubbed his face. He brushed his teeth. He shaved. He dressed.

He went out to the kitchen and made a pot of coffee and chugged most of it down black.

As he stood there with the coffee mug in his hands, he thought about how he'd come home the day before—apprehensive, nervous, wondering if he and Mariah could get past that one night.

Now he knew, with a certain bitter irony, that they'd never get past it.

So much for getting his friendship with Mariah back.

It would be better, he thought, if he didn't. If they had nothing more to do with each other. He would miss her, but everything had changed anyway.

Maybe, he thought, buoyed by coffee and desperate hopes, she would move away. She didn't have to live in the city for her work. Last summer she'd lived out in the Hamptons while her place was being renovated. Maybe she would move out there.

Then they wouldn't have to see each other any more at all.

He could get her address and send a monthly check. Do his part. He didn't think she would press him to do more.

She hadn't argued with him.

She hadn't said a word.

She understood.

He took a deep breath, felt his chest expand, felt the slightest easing of the weight that had been pressing on him since she'd said that fateful word: *pregnant.* He took another experimental breath, and then another.

Yes, he did feel better.

He flexed his shoulders. He felt slightly looser, steadier. More balanced. Like a fighter getting to his feet after a knockdown punch.

He'd been down. But he wasn't out.

He could manage. He could cope. Exactly the way he'd always coped.

Rhys finished his coffee. Then he picked up his duffel bag, carried it down to the basement and dumped everything he owned into the washing machine, exactly the way he did every time he got home.

He concentrated on it now. Focused on every movement as he measured the soap, added the bleach. Always bleach. A lot of bleach.

It made things clean again.

He needed things clean again. Neat. Under control.

He shut the lid, turned the knob and gave it a pull. The machine began to fill—the way it always did.

He hummed tunelessly as he went back upstairs—the way he always did.

He reached for the phone.

And stopped.

He'd been going to ring Mariah to see if she wanted to go grab a bite of lunch.

So, all right, some things would change.

But not the important ones, he reminded himself. He would still be on his own. Solitary. Untouched. Untouchable.

Exactly the way he wanted it.

CHAPTER THREE

MARIAH'S houseguests left on Saturday.

"It was fabulous! We had a terrific time." Erica turned from getting into the taxi that would take them to the airport and gave Mariah one last hug. "I can't thank you enough for putting up with us."

"My pleasure," Mariah assured her. And it had been—to a degree. Having Erica and Jeff and the kids there all week had kept her busy—and sane. It had kept her from wondering what Rhys was doing, if he was coming to terms with things, what was going on in his head.

She hadn't heard a word from him all week.

She'd thought he would sulk, that he would be angry, that he might even pretend she wasn't pregnant—for a while.

But she didn't think he would pretend she didn't exist.

They were *friends,* damn it! Friends didn't drop each other. Friends didn't turn their backs on each other. Friends didn't ignore another friend's very being.

But Rhys was ignoring hers.

She hadn't seen him. She hadn't heard from him. She excused him, telling herself that he didn't want to come around to talk about things further while Erica and Jeff were there. She didn't blame him. And she knew he had a lot of thinking to do.

She didn't expect it to be easy for him. She didn't expect, even when he got things sorted out in his head, that he would dote the way Gibson did or the way her other friend Izzy's husband, Finn, had when she'd been pregnant.

She didn't expect him to ask her to marry him. Not at once. Not yet.

Though deep down she did dare hope.

But at the very least she expected to see him again.

She didn't—not once all week.

Finally, the night before Erica and Jeff were going to leave, she cooked dinner for everyone and invited her sister, Sierra, and some friends Jeff and Erica had met during the week—Finn and Izzy MacCauley and Gib and Chloe Walker and Sam and Josie Fletcher. Rhys knew them all. They'd wonder why he wasn't there if she didn't invite him.

So she'd invited him. He wasn't home, so she'd left a message on his answering machine. She wasn't putting pressure on him, she assured herself. She was just being neighborly—being *a friend*.

The next morning when she came back from the grocery store, she found a message he'd left in return.

"Thank you for your invitation," Rhys said in a voice so polite and distant she almost hadn't recognized him. "But I'm afraid I have another commitment."

He was *afraid he had another commitment*?

Whatever happened to his normal, cheerful, "Can't make it for dinner. Sorry. I'll drop in when I get back"?

Mariah felt a trickle of worry skate down her spine.

Everyone else had come to dinner. They all asked about Rhys.

"He had another commitment," Mariah said, very properly quoting his words and trying not to sound sarcastic.

But Izzy and Finn's eyebrows lifted. Chloe looked astonished. Sam said, "Not overseas, is he?"

And Gib said, "What commitment is better than us?"

"He'll show up," Sierra had predicted with cheerful optimism. "Probably had some sort of family thing he couldn't get out of."

Maybe, but Mariah doubted it. She didn't think he did much except go fishing with his brothers.

In any case, he never showed up.

She felt empty. Worried. Vaguely lost. She told herself that it would take him time, that maybe he just didn't want to deal with anything while her cousin and family were still there. She gave him the benefit of the doubt.

Now, though, as she gave Erica one last hug, she saw the ornamental gate that led to his apartment open. Her heart kicked over. She gave Erica a squeeze. "Come back again. Soon."

"You come home," Erica countered as she took Ashley from Jeff.

"Sometime," Mariah promised. She was aware of Rhys locking the gate behind her.

"Oh, there's Rhys! Hi, Rhys!" Erica said.

Mariah turned to see a faint smile flicker across Rhys's face. The smile was directed at Erica. He nodded pleasantly.

"We're just leaving," Erica said. "We missed you at dinner last night."

Rhys kept his polite smile. He didn't reply. He was dressed to go jogging, and ordinarily Mariah knew he would loop an arm around her shoulder and say, "Go get some shorts on. I'll wait for you."

Now he kept his distance. Didn't even look her way.

She wetted her lips and turned back to Erica, saying cheerfully, "Have a safe trip. Bye, Ty. Bye, Jeff." She gave the baby a buss on her fat pink cheek, smiling as Ashley clapped her hands and drooled.

Out of the corner of her eye Mariah saw Rhys come up the steps. He was four feet from her. Less, as he opened the waist-high wrought-iron gate that opened onto the sidewalk. And then more.

He was moving away.

He didn't even stop. Didn't even so much as glance her way. He went right out the gate and down the street.

The taxi doors slammed, Mariah watched him go.

"Bye! Goodbye! Bye, Mariah!" Erica and Jeff and Tyler all called.

"Bye!" Mariah waved madly as the taxi drove off. Then her gaze shifted to the man striding away towards the park.

"Goodbye," she repeated softly.

But she knew it wasn't Erica, Jeff, Tyler or Ashley she was talking to.

He stayed away.

He flew out to Colorado and spent a few days with his photographer brother, Nathan. He went out to Montauk and spent a weekend fishing with his businessman brother, Dominic.

And every time he came back he saw Mariah.

She didn't make any effort to avoid him. She smiled. She said, "Hi." She looked at him with those big gray eyes that he remembered too well from the night he'd made love with her—and, in spite of himself, he wanted to do it all over again.

But, more than that, he didn't want to think about her at all.

When he was home he saw her every day. She came out on her terrace to water the plants when he was down in his back garden. She sat on the stoop and talked to Mrs. Alvarez who lived upstairs. She hung out her laundry on that ridiculous little contraption that she used to dry what she called her "delicate items."

Panties, she meant. Bras.

It drove him nuts.

He might not talk to her anymore. He might not see her face to face. But he could hardly avoid seeing a whole row of her bras flapping in the breeze. And those colorful scraps of something or other flapping beside them—had she *always* hung her panties to dry in the sun?

He'd never noticed before.

His gaze locked on the pair of peach-colored ones he remembered peeling off her.

He had half a mind to call her up and tell her to stop scandalizing the neighbors.

Fortunately he came to his senses first.

But he didn't stay in the garden. It wasn't that nice a day. He didn't need to stand out there watering shrubs. Just because it was exactly the sort of thing he most longed to do when he was halfway across the world in some land where green was an unknown color, that didn't mean he needed to do it now.

There would be time later.

When Mariah Kelly's scandalous underwear was dry and folded and put away.

He was avoiding her.

There was no other word to describe it. Mariah was a writer; she made her living using the correct words.

Avoiding. Yep, that was what he was doing. Not only wasn't he calling her or dropping by her apartment, he was heading the other way if he saw her coming. He was ducking into shops to miss her. He was going out of his way to keep out of hers.

She didn't avoid him.

Mariah had always faced life straight on. She did now. She kept right on walking when she saw him coming, and when he cut into the grocery store to avoid her she swallowed the hurt and walked on. She kept right on watering her plants or hanging out her clothes when he was in his garden. She even waved at him or called, "Hello." And when he ignored her or pretended he didn't hear she told herself he was still coming to terms.

And she believed it.

But she was getting tired of waiting.

That was the trouble with working at home. She was there too much. It was too easy to be snubbed when it seemed that sitting around waiting to be snubbed was all you did all day—even if you were really writing articles.

She needed to get out—get away—do another personality piece. She'd been skipping those assignments recently because she couldn't predict how her stomach would behave. It was usually all right by late morning, but she couldn't get up early and head off for an interview if she was going to be upchucking all the way.

She didn't know how much longer Stella, her boss, was going to tolerate her saying no, though. Stella didn't know she was pregnant.

No one knew—except Rhys.

Soon she would have to tell everyone. But not yet. Every day she told herself, Not yet.

The phone rang that evening at suppertime. She'd given up hoping it would be Rhys. Well, she'd almost given up. Her heart still beat faster every time the phone rang. But she didn't snatch it up the way she had at first. Now she let it ring three times before she grabbed it.

It was Stella. "Have I got an interview for you!"

"Interview? When? Where? I don't know if I can get away right now," Mariah began cautiously.

"You will for this one. It's Sloan Gallagher."

"Sloan Gallagher? He doesn't give interviews," Mariah reminded her. No one had been granted an interview with the reclusive box office idol in years. No one even knew exactly where he lived. If they did, the world would be camping on his doorstep. As it was, Sloan Gallagher covered his tracks so well that the world didn't know where his doorstep was.

"Sand Gap, Montana," Stella told her. "And he wants to talk to *you!*"

"Me? I never asked to interview him."

"No, but everyone else always is. And he wants to do his bit to promote this new picture of his—cares about it like he's never cared about any of the others, apparently—so he's agreed to an interview. With you."

"Why me?"

"He says you're fair. You're sensible. He read the piece you did on Gavin McConnell and he was impressed, so he called."

Gavin McConnell, another of Hollywood's more reluctant interviewees, had talked to Mariah last fall. The article had run last month.

"*He* called *you*?"

"Believe it or not." Stella was clearly in awe. "He wants you to come to his ranch. To be there for the round-up…and the branding. To portray him as he really is, not the way Hollywood thinks he is."

"The round-up? The branding? Gallagher brands cattle? He really *ranches*?" There had been rumors to that effect, but Mariah had passed them off as just that—rumors.

"Apparently. That's what he's invited you to come and find out. Figure on a week."

"A week?"

"He's offered a week. Surely you're not going to want to do it in less?" Stella sounded as if she would doubt Mariah's sanity if she did.

Mariah wasn't sure she was going to do it at all. What if she upchucked all over Sloan Gallagher's ranch?

But if she stayed home, what good would that do? She'd just sit here and fret about Rhys. And maybe, being on site, she could pick her moments, avoid having to be in interview mode when her nausea was at its worst.

"All right," she told Stella. "I'll go."

*   *   *

She was everywhere he looked.

And then one day she wasn't there.

Rhys rejoiced. He watered his shrubs, smiling when he didn't see her on her terrace. No underwear flapped in the breeze, either. Another plus.

He went jogging in the park and didn't catch a glimpse of her. He sat in his living room and read the *Times* and never saw her once go up or down the stairs. He even lingered on the stoop and talked to Mrs. Alvarez for half an hour or so that evening, and relished the fact that Mariah wasn't there.

She didn't show her face the next day, either.

He supposed she was out of town doing an interview. She was often gone a day or two. When her subjects didn't live in the city, he knew she went to them.

Sometimes she went to the Hamptons, sometimes to Greenwich or the Cape, sometimes to Martha's Vineyard or to Bucks County or occasionally even farther afield.

The magazine she wrote for had national coverage, but she tended to get the assignments that were based in the northeast. Ordinarily he would have known where she'd gone. She would have told him.

Mrs. Alvarez would know. He should ask Mrs. Alvarez.

Like hell!

The thought brought him up short. He didn't care where she was. It didn't matter to him. It wasn't as if he really wanted to know. And it wasn't as if he had any vested interest in the answer.

They had only been friends.

Now they were…less.

He went out to the new Thai place on Broadway for dinner by himself. Mariah loved Thai food. He wondered if she'd tried it.

Then he did his best not to think of her again for the rest of the night.

Maybe when he saw her tomorrow he'd ask her. Casually. No need to snub her completely, after all. He just needed to keep his distance, not let her depend on him emotionally. Not get involved.

But Mariah wasn't there the next day, either.

Or the day after that.

When he didn't see her for the fifth straight day, he began to wonder. And that annoyed him, too, because he didn't want to wonder.

"Then ask," he growled at himself.

Mrs. Alvarez would tell him. She would give him a knowing look and say, "She's in East Hampton interviewing that sexy leading man," or, "She's in Newport with that handsome sailor," hoping to make him jealous.

She always hoped that. She thought he and Mariah were "made for each other."

Of course that wasn't true.

Rhys was made for no one, and he was never jealous.

But at least he would have known.

Not that it made any difference. He wasn't going to suggest they go to the Thai place. Or to a Yankees game. He went to one without her. He went to Lincoln Plaza to see a new film, too.

He barely grunted a greeting at Mrs. Alvarez as he left to go jogging that evening. She was sitting on the stoop, watching for a delivery man.

He didn't like the way she looked at him when he passed. Closely. Curiously. Speculatively?

Had Mariah told her about the baby? Had she guessed?

Mariah didn't show yet. But it wouldn't be long until she did. What would she look like when her belly was big with child?

The thought made Rhys stumble on the bottom step.

"You watch yourself there," Mrs. Alvarez said.

Rhys didn't answer. He hauled himself up and shoved the thought of Mariah away.

He didn't care. Didn't want to know!

Sarah had been four months along when...

No! He started to run toward the park. He wouldn't think about that, either. Wouldn't let himself remember. He picked up speed, dodged around a pedestrian, sprinted across Columbus.

He did more than jog around the reservoir. He ran.

Mrs. Alvarez was still on the stoop an hour later when he staggered back, sweating and gasping for breath. "You run like all the demons in hell are after you," she said.

Rhys thought that pretty much summed it up.

On the eighth day, he spotted her getting out of a taxi.

Rhys had just rounded the corner, coming home from an early evening run—he'd stopped calling them jogs. And, even though he'd hit the wall metaphorically just minutes before, he sprinted to grab Mariah's arm before he got to the door.

"Where the hell have you been?" The words were out before he could stop them—or even give them any thought.

She stared at him. She looked tired, he thought. And surprised.

So was he. Hastily he dropped her arm and stepped back. "People have asked," he explained gruffly.

Mariah's eyebrow arched. "People?"

"Chloe." Which wasn't entirely true, but might well be.

Chloe Walker had lived in Mariah's apartment last summer while it was being renovated. She'd gone out with Rhys occasionally while Mariah was staying out in the Hamptons. Then last autumn, instead of going home to Iowa to marry her fiancé, she'd married Gibson Walker, the photographer she'd come to work for, instead.

Now Chloe was pregnant, too. Big as a house. She

looked as if she was taking in tenants. Rhys had run into her, literally, at Zabar's two days ago. She'd said, "We missed you at Mariah's the other night."

And he'd mumbled something about being busy.

In fact he'd gone down to a jazz club in SoHo just to be out of the house when all of Mariah's guests had come. He hadn't wanted to go to her place and have dinner, hadn't wanted to see anyone, to pretend that nothing had changed. He didn't want to answer questions if they knew—or to feel awkward if they didn't.

"Another time," Chloe had said cheerfully. "We'll have you guys over. After the baby's born. Say hi to Mariah."

That was as good as asking after her.

"She said she hadn't talked to you since your dinner," Rhys told Mariah now. "And she wondered where you were."

"Montana. I had an assignment out there."

He was surprised. She never went that far from home as a rule. He wanted to ask about it. He always enjoyed hearing about her interviews, liked to find out her take on the rich and famous. Mariah understood people better than anyone he knew. She empathized. She got inside their skin. She made them come alive for him.

But he didn't ask.

He picked up her suitcase off the ground before she could. "I'll carry it up for you," he said brusquely.

He told himself he should have just let her go up by herself. But the suitcase looked heavy. She probably shouldn't be carrying anything that bulky. Not in her...condition. He tried not to look at her midsection. Tried not to notice if she was "showing."

She led the way. Rhys followed.

She was silent as she opened the door and started up the steps, but then she started talking, telling him about her interview. When she mentioned Sloan Gallagher, his eyebrows went up. Even he knew Gallagher didn't give interviews. He was curious how she'd managed to talk Hollywood's most sought after, most reluctant star into speaking to her.

He didn't ask.

He just clamped his mouth shut and went up the stairs behind her.

It was a memorable view.

In fact, the sight of Mariah's curvy bottom in a pair of linen trousers on eye level for two flights almost did him in. Winded from his run anyway and annoyed at his reaction to her, by the time he got to her door Rhys was gasping for air.

Mariah turned to look at him. "Out of shape?" she asked, and he didn't think she was joking.

He didn't answer. Couldn't without wheezing. So he just waited while she unlocked the door to her flat and, when she had, he followed her in and put the suitcase down.

"Thank you." She smiled at him. "Would you like a glass of iced water?" She sounded cheerful, glad to see him, as if nothing had changed.

But it had. He shook his head. "No." He turned toward the door. "Gotta go."

She blinked in surprise. Her smiled faltered, then faded.

He did his best not to notice. "See you," he muttered and went down the stairs two at a time.

He wondered if it was just wishful thinking that heard her say, "Not if I see you first."

So much for hopes.

She'd gone away telling herself that not being there expecting to hear from him would help—both of them. She wouldn't be jumping up at every moment hoping the phone or the doorbell was him. He would have time to come to terms with the news.

She'd come home believing that he would have done so.

She'd come home ready to open her arms to him, to rejoice with him, to agree that, while this might not have been the best way to start a family, it was going to be all right, that they would make it—the three of them.

And when he'd come running to grab her suitcase it had been all she could do not to embrace him right then.

Good thing she hadn't, she told herself.

Otherwise she'd have been kicking herself now—wishing she'd shown a little restraint.

Because Rhys was apparently nowhere near ready to accept the news of his impending fatherhood. He was nowhere near ready to want to be a part of this miracle of new life that he and she had begun.

He might never be ready.

It was the first time she'd actually let herself think that thought.

Her mind—and her heart—almost instantly rejected it. She loved Rhys. She didn't want to believe he would turn his back on that love—or on their child.

"But it's possible," she told herself, staring in the mirror, studying her naked body which seemed already to be changing shape. She was almost three months along now. Getting bigger, rounder.

And still getting nauseated, though not as often or as severely. It usually took something yucky to set it off—like the time Sloan Gallagher had offered her a taste of what he called a "Rocky Mountain Oyster" for breakfast.

She'd looked at it dubiously. "A what?"

"A testicle," he'd told her.

She'd made a run for the bathroom.

Later, to regain her credibility, she'd had to explain—to tell him it wasn't simply female squeamishness that had sent her running with her hand over her mouth, but a certain "condition" her body was in.

She'd been embarrassed, felt vulnerable. He'd been gentle and kind and surprisingly supportive and understanding. For a hard-edged roughneck like Sloan Gallagher was reputed to be, she was amazed. And impressed. It gave her more fodder for her article she was calling "Would the real Sloan Gallagher please stand up?"

Stella would love it.

And a good thing, too, Mariah told herself. Since it looked as if she was going to be a single mother.

"He said he'd help financially," she reminded herself.

And he probably would. But finances were the least of her problems. Mariah might not be rich, but she was doing fine financially on her own. And she expected to continue doing fine even after she had the baby.

It wasn't in the financial area that she wanted Rhys's support.

It was in her life—in the baby's life.

But she wasn't going to beg.

She smiled at him when she saw him. She talked to him when she ran into him on the stairs. She waited for some sign that he was coming around.

And she kept right on waiting.

"A baby shower?" Rhys almost swallowed his tongue. He stared aghast at the phone in his hand. "*Whose* baby shower?"

"Chloe's, of course," Izzy MacCauley said cheerfully. "Who else do you know who's going to have a baby?"

Realizing that the question was rhetorical, Rhys breathed a little easier. "Men don't go to baby showers," he told Izzy, who had just invited him. "They're for girls."

"Nonsense. Gib and Finn will be here. And Sam Fletcher. You've met Sam." Izzy wasn't the sort to take no for an answer and he knew it.

"All right," Rhys told her. "I'll come."

"Great. Why don't you come with Mariah?"

"I can't!"

"Why not?"

"I'm…" he cast about desperately for a reason "…going fishing with my brother that day. I don't know when we'll be back."

"Okay," Izzy said. "We're just glad you're coming. We missed you at Mariah's party."

"Mmm," Rhys said.

She hung up.

He made the mistake of telling Dominic about the baby shower while they were fishing. "It's not a big deal," he said. "I can miss it if we get back late." *Please, let's get back late.*

But Dominic just grinned. "Baby shower? Hell of a social life you've got. Wouldn't want you to miss that."

Dominic made sure they were back. He even volunteered to take care of putting the fish in the freezer while Rhys cleaned up and went to the MacCauleys'.

Giving him a sour look, Rhys left him to it.

He took his time showering and shaving. He had second and third thoughts about going at all. What if Mariah had told everyone?

What the hell was he walking into?

"Have fun," Dominic grinned when he left.

"Oh, yeah," Rhys said. "Oh, yeah."

Everyone was already there when he arrived.

"Come on in." Tansy and Pansy, Finn and Izzy's nieces, drew him in. "Everybody's out on the terrace." They led him through the airy, high-ceilinged living room and out onto the terrace in back where a dozen people laughed and chatted.

He only saw one.

Mariah.

Actually he saw two, he realized a second later. She was

sitting on the glider bouncing Finn and Izzy's younger son, Crash, on her lap. As the glider swayed back and forth, Mariah held ten-month-old Crash's hands, and let him dance on her knees. They were both laughing, and she looked like…like a mother.

It knocked Rhys for a loop.

He'd never thought of Mariah like that.

He'd seen her around kids, but he'd never considered her having any. And now…now he stared…until she looked up and noticed him. Then quickly he looked away.

"Can I get you something to drink?" Finn asked him. "Beer? Iced tea?"

"Beer," Rhys muttered. He was tempted to ask for Scotch. Neat.

He drank his beer. He stayed away from Mariah. It was clear she hadn't told anyone about her pregnancy. Everyone was busy hovering around Chloe, patting her belly and recalling when Izzy had been that big.

No one mentioned that in a few short months Mariah would be that size as well.

Rhys gulped his beer and tried to blot the image from his mind.

"Can I get you another?" Finn asked him.

He said, "Sure."

He talked to Finn and Gib about the time he'd spent in Colorado with Nathan. Finn envied Nathan his niche as a wildlife photographer. Both he and Gib specialized in other areas of the field, but were always eager to talk about related topics.

He talked to Sam Fletcher and Damon Alexakis, both importers and friends of Izzy and Finn, about the Far East. Sam had just come back from Singapore. Damon had just returned from Greece. Rhys had been in both places in the past year when he'd been overseas teaching or putting out fires.

He talked to Tansy and Pansy and to Izzy. He watched Mariah the whole night.

She looked marvelous. There was a glow about her. He'd noticed it the minute he'd come through the door and spied her with Finn and Izzy's baby in her arms. She was comfortable with Crash. She doted on him and he responded to her.

Which was good, he told himself, because she'd need just such competence in not very many months.

Then, as he watched, Finn came over and scooped Crash out of her arms. "Take a break," he told her. "He's imposed on you enough."

"I don't mind," Mariah said.

"You would," Finn told her, "if you had to do it all the time."

And Rhys began to notice how true that was. Finn and Izzy worked as a team dealing with the twins and with Crash and his older brother, two-year-old Rip. Sam and Josie Fletcher did the same with their son, Jake. Even Chloe wasn't coping on her own. Gib was hovering—bringing her a plate of food, getting her a cushion to put behind her back. He was always there for her.

It made Rhys think.

Mariah shouldn't have to go it alone.

She would need support. Sending her a check every month wasn't going to be enough.

One single parent wasn't going to be enough.

He never said a word to her all evening. He talked to everyone else. All the men. Every woman but her. And Chloe.

It occurred to her later that he'd never talked to Chloe.

Was he allergic to all pregnant women, then?

Mariah didn't know. She tried not to be irritated. She tried not to care. It wasn't easy, especially when, as she was leaving, Izzy said to Rhys, "Are you going now, too?"

He shook his head. "No," he said. "I'll stick around."
Izzy looked surprised.

Mariah tried not to. "I don't need an escort," she said briskly. She thanked Izzy and Finn for the party, gave Chloe and Gib one last hug and more good wishes. She said goodnight to everyone else. She didn't even look at Rhys.

She didn't know if Izzy or Chloe or anyone else noticed.

She didn't care.

She went home and went to bed.

But she didn't sleep. She tossed and turned and fumed and fretted. She rubbed her belly and wondered about the child inside. Seeing Chloe tonight had brought things home to her. Right now her child was almost an abstraction. She couldn't even feel it yet. But it wouldn't be long until she was as ungainly as Chloe was now. And in a little more than a year she would have a child the size of Crash.

Another person.

Needing her.

Would she be enough? Would she be able to cope?

Of course she would.

But in the middle of the night it was hard to feel as confident as she did in the bright light of a summer afternoon.

Fortunately it was a bright summer afternoon and she was working on an article and feeling much more in control and competent when the buzzer on her door sounded.

She expected Mrs. Alvarez, who had said she would bring Mariah back a carton of milk when she returned from the grocery store.

But when she opened the door it was Rhys who was standing there.

"Hey."

She smiled a little cautiously this time. He smiled a little, too. She felt her hopes gather once more. Maybe he'd thought about parenthood, too, after last night. Maybe it had been the wake-up call he needed. Maybe he didn't say anything last night because he wanted to wait until they were alone. Her smile widened somewhat.

Rhys scratched the back of his head and shifted from one foot to the other as if he was nervous. But then he said, "I came to talk. Do you have a minute?"

She nodded and opened the door farther. "Do you want to sit down? I can make some iced tea."

"No. Thanks," he added after a moment. He walked to the end of the living room, then turned and faced her.

"I've been thinking," he began finally. "About you. About your being…pregnant." He paused.

She nodded, encouraging him.

"Last night made me think. Seeing Gib with Chloe and Finn with Izzy and Sam and Josie and all of 'em made me think."

Mariah nodded again. Her heart beat faster. "Yes."

"It looks like it takes two," he said. "No matter what they say about single parenting being okay—and it is if you can't get anything better, I guess—it's still not the ideal. The ideal is two parents." He looked at her, then down at his feet, then out the window.

"Yes," Mariah said. Then, "Yes," more firmly, more loudly. "I agree."

"You're gonna need emotional support. Moral support. Not just financial."

Thank God, Mariah thought. Oh, thank you, God.

Rhys rubbed the back of his neck. "That's what I've been thinking about. I can do the financial. But the other…I know it's important." He cast a quick glance at her to see and she stared at him, not following.

"Yes," she said again. *Been here, done this,* she thought. "What are you saying?"

Rhys jammed his hands into the pockets of his jeans and

rocked on his heels. "Well, like I said, it's important—that a kid have two parents. Two people to take care of him. And you're gonna need somebody, too. So I was thinking…you need to find somebody. A guy, I mean."

She felt her jaw drop.

"And I wanted you to know I wouldn't mind…if you found somebody. Some guy. To have a relationship. To marry you." He looked at her as if he expected her to say thank you.

She couldn't say a word. Still. Her mind was in a whirl. She couldn't believe what she was hearing.

"You're a great woman, Mariah. Pretty. Smart. Sensitive. You could probably have any guy you wanted. Even being pregnant. I know some guys aren't keen on raising another guy's kid. But whoever you picked…well, you could tell him he wouldn't have to worry about the money. I'll do that. I told you I would. So he wouldn't be stuck, if you know what I mean. With expenses." He sounded a little desperate now, as if he was tacking words on as they came to him, as if he wasn't sure they made any sense, but he needed to say something.

Mariah managed to shut her mouth.

"Well?" Rhys said irritably. "What do you think?"

She found her voice. She jerked open the door and held it wide. "I think," she said through her teeth, "that you can go to hell, Rhys Wolfe. Get out!"

CHAPTER FOUR

LIKE she would just go out and lasso a husband and drag him home!

So some total stranger could take care of her—and some other man's baby!

No, not a man! As far as Mariah was concerned, Rhys Wolfe didn't qualify as a man. Not even close! What a jerk!

How dared he suggest such a thing?

"You know I'm right, Mariah," he said as she practically slammed the door against his backside as he went out.

"The hell I do." And she threw a book at the door while she could still hear his footsteps on the stairs. Then she called him every vile name she could think of.

Finally she burst into tears.

It was the first time she'd cried.

Since she'd discovered she was pregnant, she'd thrown up. She'd been panic-stricken. She'd talked herself silly and worried herself sick.

But she hadn't cried—until now.

It was hormones, she assured herself.

It wasn't Rhys. Rhys wasn't worth crying over.

But still the tears fell. Tears of frustration, of anger, of pure fury. Tears of misunderstanding and betrayal, of lost hope and shattered dreams. She cried until she was spent.

And then she said to herself, "Buck up." She wiped her eyes and blew her nose. She straightened up and made herself stare at her reflection in the mirror.

A blotchy-faced thirty-one-year-old woman stared back.

A woman with red eyes, a red nose and disheveled long brown hair. A woman who was by no stretch of the imagination pretty. She couldn't imagine one man being thrilled to have her—let alone the droves of them Rhys seemed to think would be delighted.

Rhys didn't know what he was talking about.

He was wrong about her being smart, too. If she were, she wouldn't have got herself into this fix.

Sensitive? Well, yes, she'd give him that once. It was because she'd been sensitive to his pain that she was expecting Rhys's child.

Her child. Not *his*. He didn't want it. The more fool he.

She cupped her slightly rounded belly. "Guess it's just you and me, kiddo." She tried to muster a watery smile. It was a struggle. She made herself stand there and look in the mirror until she was satisfied with it—satisfied that she looked strong and confident and brave.

She stood there a very long time.

And while she was there she realized it wasn't just her and the baby. She had friends. She had family. She would have support—as soon as she filled them in.

As it happened, her sister Sierra turned up on her doorstep the next morning before she had a chance.

Mariah had got up early, determined to get her life on track, to begin as she meant to go on. She'd ended up in the bathroom with her head over the toilet, plagued by the morning sickness that the doctor promised would soon go away.

It couldn't be soon enough for her, Mariah had thought wearily and, clutching a cup of tea and a packet of soda crackers, she had gone back to bed.

She'd stayed there until close to eleven. Lying on her back, reading a book, scribbling notes for an upcoming article, chastising her incipient child for the inconvenience.

And the doorbell rang.

She had a momentary qualm that it would be Rhys, then

decided she didn't care if it was. She was still a little queasy. She'd just make sure she aimed for his shoes. Smiling wanly at the thought, she opened the door.

"Well, don't let me get you up," Sierra said, eyeing her sister's tousled hair and oversized T-shirt that had obviously been slept in. "You look frowsier than I do." Sierra's spiky purple hair, spandex top and baggy khakis were all calculated, though.

"I'm working," Mariah lied. "I just didn't comb my hair."

"Or get dressed." Sierra clearly didn't believe a word of it. She brushed past Mariah into the living room, then turned and regarded her sister frankly and appraisingly. "You know, I just noticed—you're getting boobs."

"What!" Instinctively Mariah slapped her arms across her breasts and fixed her sister with a glare. She didn't know what Sierra was doing here in the middle of the morning anyway, but she couldn't believe her sister had come to check on the size of her breasts.

An odd smell emanating from the bag in one of Sierra's hands was making her feel a little queasy again.

Sierra shrugged amiably. "Well, it could be that I don't often see you braless in a T-shirt. But I really think you are." She moved Mariah's arms away from her unfettered breasts. "About time. What are you now? Thirty-two?"

"Thirty-*one,*" Mariah corrected her frostily.

"Whatever. If it can happen to you, I can pretend it's not too late for me." Sierra looked down, disgusted at her own nearly flat chest banded in Day-Glo orange. "How'd you do it?"

"I—" *I'm not going to answer that,* Mariah thought. What *was* that smell?

"What's the no bra bit?" Sierra asked. "You becoming a feminist? Developing some political gender consciousness?"

Mariah sighed and raked her fingers through her hair. "I wasn't going anywhere so I didn't bother."

"One of the joys of getting to work at home," Sierra agreed. "I envy you that. And your bigger boobs."

Would Sierra envy her sister the reason for her bigger breasts? Mariah wondered. She swayed a little and grabbed the back of a chair for support. "What are you doing here?"

"We just finished up a shoot in the park," Sierra said cheerfully, "and since I was in the neighborhood and I hadn't seen you in a while I stopped at O'Toole's and brought lunch." She thrust the brown paper bag she'd been carrying into Mariah's hands. "Your favorite."

The smell. *Please, God, no. Don't let it be—*

"Corned beef and cabbage." Sierra beamed, then gaped as Mariah dropped the bag and bolted. "Mariah? *Mariah!*"

But Mariah was already in the bathroom, parting company with the tea and soda crackers.

Her sister banged on the door. "*Mariah?* Are you all right?"

"'M f-fine," Mariah managed as soon as she could get a breath. She slumped back on the cold tile, leaned against the tub and let her head drop forward between her knees. Her brain was doing slow, lazy rolls between her ears. Her stomach was trying to get a foothold somewhere in the middle of her guts.

"Have you got the flu?" Sierra demanded. "Is that why you were still in bed?"

"No." Mariah struggled up. She stood hanging on to the sink, taking deep desperate breaths.

"Mariah!"

"I'm okay." Three more deep breaths and Mariah washed her face. Then she brushed her teeth and tried to slap some color into her cheeks.

She took a ragged breath and told herself she was fine.

She *was* fine. This was normal. But she couldn't open the door. Not until… "Could you, er, maybe take that… um…bag…outside?"

"Done."

Mariah heard her sister's footsteps retreat. She heard the front door open.

She took a deep breath and then another. "Fine," she repeated. "I'm fine." Just in case her stomach needed to hear it to be convinced.

When she opened the door, Sierra was just coming back in, concern wreathing her face. She studied Mariah carefully, eyes narrow, head tilted, not speaking.

The two of them looked at each other. Finally Mariah frowned. "What?"

Sierra shook her head as if she'd thought of something, then rejected it. But then her gaze narrowed further. "Big boobs. Baggy T-shirts. Ralphing at the smell of corned beef. Mariah, are you *pregnant*?"

And Mariah wrapped her arms across her middle again and met Sierra's blue gaze defiantly. "What if I am?"

"Oh, my God." Sierra's eyes almost popped out of her head. Her jaw sagged. "You are.'

"So?" Mariah hugged herself tighter. "It's not necessarily a bad thing!"

"No, of course not! I just never thought it would be you who… I mean…" Sierra shook her head again, this time as if to clear it. "You were always the…" She didn't finish that sentence either.

It didn't matter. Mariah knew what she'd been going to say.

You were always the Goody Two-Shoes in the family. The one who never misstepped, who never colored outside the lines.

And it was true, she hadn't.

Free-spirited, Day-Glo Sierra had done enough of that

for both of them! And both sisters knew that, if a Kelly daughter were going to get pregnant in a less than acceptable situation, Sierra would have been the one expected to do it.

"Well," Sierra said now, blinking rapidly and not seeming to know what to do with her hands. She pasted on a bright smile. "This will take some getting used to. Who's the lucky dad?"

"Never mind."

"Never mind?" Sierra stared. Then, ignoring the quelling look Mariah gave her, she demanded, "Does he know?"

"He knows."

"And?"

Mariah gave her best negligent, disinterested shrug and tossed her head. "He's not interested."

"What kind of idiot did you—?"

"He's not an idiot! Well, maybe he is." Yes, he definitely was. "He just…doesn't want to be a father."

"He should have thought of that before," Sierra said acidly.

"Drop it. Just…drop it, Sierra."

"But—"

"Drop it."

Sierra didn't look as if she was going to. Her mouth opened, then closed. She leaned against the wall and took a deep breath, then let it out. Finally she dropped it, only to change tack and ask, "Do the folks know?"

"No one knows. But him. And now you."

Sierra digested that. A worried look crossed her face. "You're not…not thinking about not having…"

"No, I'm not! I intend to have this baby! And I'm going to keep him. Or her. There has never been any question about that!" She glared at her sister for even thinking such a thing.

"Right," Sierra agreed quickly. "I didn't really think..." Of course she wouldn't. She knew Mariah. One mistake would not be compounded by another far worse. Sierra scratched her head. She jammed her hands in those baggy pants that looked as if they might fall right off her narrow hips. She took one deep breath, and then another, coming to terms.

Finally she rubbed her hands together briskly. "Well, good," she said with a grin. "I've always wanted to be an aunt. How can I help?"

Mariah blinked, her lashes suddenly damp. She flung her arms around her sister. "You just did." She hadn't realized how important her sister's support would be until she had it. "Thank you."

Sierra gave her a hard hug. "My pleasure. You knew I would. You've always been there for me."

It was true. Mariah had always been there, defending her little sister's right to be different. To spike her hair and dye it green or pink or purple. To wear Day-Glo and spandex with her Doc Martens boots when the rest of Kansas wore blue jeans.

She'd stuck up for Sierra's right to have a boyfriend with a tattoo on his nose, too. And for the one with the Harley and the chains and the gold-capped teeth.

Sierra gave her one last squeeze, then stepped back and looked down at Mariah's abdomen. "There is a hint," she said thoughtfully. "And not just the boobs. You're getting a tummy. And you've got a glow," she said, studying her sister's face. "Now that you're not barfing, you look, well, radiant." She smiled again. "So when's it due?"

"Six months."

Sierra did the math on her fingers. "A Christmas baby?"

Mariah nodded. "That's what the doctor says."

"Well, that will be a novel excuse not to go home for Christmas. Mom and Dad can come here."

"Do you think they would?" Mariah said sceptically. Their farmer parents gave New York City as wide a berth as possible.

"Count on it. You know how bad Mom wants to be a grandma."

"But under the circumstances…"

"They want our lives to be perfect, but they'll just be thrilled we're alive and well and that you're giving them a grandchild. They'll be here," Sierra predicted.

And Mariah took heart. Her parents were the salt of the earth. It was true, what Sierra said. They might wish Mariah had got pregnant under different circumstances, but she dared hope her parents would be supportive and welcome their first grandchild into their hearts.

"Can you eat anything?" Sierra asked now, getting back to practicalities. "I'm starving. We started work at five."

Mariah smiled ruefully. "And I made you ditch your lunch."

"Doesn't matter. You've got crackers? And peanut butter?" Sierra was already heading for the kitchen.

Mariah followed. "I live on crackers. The doctor said the nausea will wear off soon, and it's already getting better." She sat while Sierra made them both a stack of peanut butter and crackers. Then her sister opened cans of ginger ale and cut a shiny red apple into dainty wedges and set it on a plate. Then she put it all on the table and sat down opposite Mariah.

Mariah ate one cracker. She drank a little of the ginger ale. She ate another cracker, chewing stolidly. Sierra watched her warily and silently. Only when Mariah smiled and didn't bolt for the bathroom did her sister breathe a sigh of relief.

"Whew. So can you come to the Yankees game with Jeremy and me tonight?"

Mariah blinked. "What?"

"Well, if you're not contagious…" Sierra shrugged. "Jeremy got tickets."

Jeremy, the Boyfriend of the Month, was a personal trainer to, among others, professional athletes and Broadway stars. "Four box seats, third base side, right behind the dugout," Sierra tempted her. "What do you say?"

"Um…"

"You can bring a friend. How about the father of your child?"

"No."

"All right. Bring Rhys."

The cracker choked her. *"No!"* Desperately Mariah swallowed her vehemence—and the cracker. She coughed desperately. Sierra whacked her on the back.

"Okay now?" Sierra looked at her worriedly. "Why not Rhys? He's come with us before."

Eyes watering, still trying to catch her breath, Mariah shook her head. "I just…don't want…Rhys."

"I thought you and he were…" Her voice trailed off. Her gaze narrowed. She tilted her head and considered her sister speculatively.

Mariah tried to ignore it. She shrugged. "I just don't want him."

Sierra shrugged. "Fine. All right. No Rhys. You can take the ticket and invite somebody else." She dug in her pocket and thrust the ticket at Mariah.

"I don't know anyone—"

"Or not," Sierra said, brooking no arguments. "But you're coming."

"I—"

She fixed Mariah with the same challenging stare she'd had since they were little girls back in Emporia. "Dare you."

Well, of course there was no choice after that.

*   *   *

Rhys was hosing off the front stoop when Sierra came out the front door.

He'd always liked Mariah's sister, even though he was glad Mariah herself didn't go for international orange Day-Glo, Doc Martens, and purple body parts.

He stopped hosing and grinned at her. "Hey, Sierra. How's it going?"

"You bastard," she said. Her Doc Marten nailed him in the shin.

The trouble with living in the garden apartment was that a guy could always see what was going on. He could sit there trying to watch the news after the Yankees game and notice people coming and going to the apartments upstairs.

He could tell without even trying who they were.

He could hear a feminine laugh and know it immediately. Mariah always sounded so happy, so upbeat when she laughed. Then he heard another eager female talking and recognized Sierra's breathy voice. He didn't know the masculine voice of the third person waiting on the stoop while Mariah fished for her key. He supposed he was Sierra's date.

Nice of Sierra to take Mariah along when she went out on a date.

Nice to know Sierra had a redeeming feature, Rhys thought sourly, rubbing his shin, still sore from its encounter with her boot that afternoon.

He'd wondered if she knew. He knew now.

Outside he heard Sierra say "home run," and the guy say "bottom of the ninth." Mariah said, "Incredible. Fantastic. Perfect."

So they'd been at the game. And she hadn't asked him to come along.

Not that he expected her to. Or wanted her to. He didn't.

It was just, damn it, it was the sort of thing they used to do together!

He'd taken her to her first major league ball game three years ago. He'd introduced her to the Yankees, for heaven's sake!

And now she was going without him.

You should be glad, he reminded himself. Maybe she'd meet a man. Hell, maybe she'd meet a Yankee. Maybe some hotshot ballplayer would sweep her off her feet, carry her away and marry her, become the father for her child.

The thought didn't make him as happy as it ought to have.

Mariah was glad Sierra had made her go to the game.

It made her focus on something besides herself.

Of course she'd focused on her work over the past three months, but she hadn't really had much of a social life since she'd discovered she was pregnant. She'd gone to lunch with Chloe or she'd had dinner with Finn and Izzy.

But she'd never been able to relax, to let her hair down, to be herself. Not completely. Because she'd always been waiting for Rhys.

"Not worth waiting for," Sierra had said flatly. When they were at the game, out of the blue she added, "If you want, I'll kick him in the ass."

Mariah had laughed. It was the first time she'd laughed in months.

"I did kick him in the shin," Sierra told her.

Mariah gasped. Then laughed. "You didn't!" she protested, half horrified, half thinking it served him right.

"I certainly did," Sierra said indignantly. "I don't know why I ever thought he was a nice guy."

"He's doing what he can," Mariah said. She knew that—even as she admitted how much it personally hurt.

Sierra snorted. "You can say that when he says he doesn't want anything to do with you and the baby?"

"He'll support it financially."

"Big deal. The courts would make him do that anyway. He's a jerk," Sierra said. "You need a better man."

"That's what he said."

Sierra stared. "Rhys told you to find another man?"

Mariah nodded. "To be supportive personally. He saw Gib and Chloe, and Finn and Izzy, and he thinks I'll need that."

Sierra hadn't said anything for a moment. Then she just shook her head slowly. "I'm not sure kicking him is going to be enough."

Sierra never did anything by halves.

"I've decided Rhys is right," she informed Mariah the following evening as she strode into the apartment with a list in her hand. "So I've made up a list of guys for you."

"What?" Mariah, who was usually one step behind when it came to keeping up with Sierra's machinations on her own behalf, was completely at sea now. "What are you talking about?"

"About finding you a man."

"I don't want a man!"

"Nonsense. These are all very nice men. Lo-o-o-ovely men." Sierra drew out the word, making it sound delicious, smacking her lips at the end. "And they're eager—very eager—to meet you." She grinned.

Mariah's eyes narrowed suspiciously. "What are you up to?"

Sierra got her butter-wouldn't-melt-in-my-mouth look on her face. "Me? Nothing? Just helping out."

"I don't think so," Mariah said. She took the list out of Sierra's hand and scanned it. "Who are these guys?" She half expected a list of Sierra's ex-boyfriends. She didn't recognize a single name.

"Guys I know," Sierra said easily. She took the list back. "Damien is coming by tonight. He'll go to dinner with us. Then tomorrow you can have lunch with Kent. Brandon will take you to the concert at Carnegie Hall on Saturday—"

"Whoa! Wait. Stop. What are you doing?"

"Doing what Rhys wants," Sierra said piously. An unholy light glinted in her eyes. "Come on, Mariah. You'll have a good time."

"I don't want—"

"You want Rhys." Clearly Sierra had figured that much out. "And you aren't getting him. So you have to move on."

"I don't—"

"You have to move on, Mariah." Sierra was glaring at her sister. "Trust me."

Their gazes met. Held. Years of sisterly battles and friendship and support and devotion were in those looks. Finally Mariah nodded.

"Damien tonight," Sierra said. "Be ready at seven."

He'd told her to go out, but he didn't mean every damn night.

After her night out at the Yankees game he figured she'd stay home. He knew Mariah—she was no social butterfly. She had friends, but she didn't live in a social whirl.

Or she hadn't.

Now she was the busiest damn bee in the hive.

Every time Rhys turned around, she was going out the door on some new guy's arm. At first he'd figured they were Sierra's boyfriends—now there was a woman in a social whirl—but Sierra kept showing up with the same guy—some longhaired geek. The other guys were the ones hanging all over Mariah.

And she wasn't fighting them off, either!

He'd told her to find a man, but he hadn't figured she'd put out a general casting call and just start auditioning them. What the hell did she know about these guys? They could be ax murderers! Rapists!

She didn't have to look so damn pleased every time he saw her with them, either. They couldn't all be that charming.

She was out until all hours, too. Ten-thirty! Eleven o'clock! Didn't a woman in her condition need sleep?

Rhys sure as hell wasn't getting any—not when he was pacing around half the night waiting for her.

He needed to get away. He needed a break.

So when his brother Nathan called and wondered if he'd like to go to Vancouver for a week he jumped at the chance. Nathan was a wildlife photographer of some repute. More footloose than Rhys had ever been—because he'd never been married, never even been close—Nathan traveled all over the world doing photos for articles and, more recently, books of his own.

Like Rhys, Nathan had turned his back on the family business long ago, though for far less obvious reasons. No one in the family knew why one day Nathan had been there, and the next he'd taken off.

No one asked.

Nathan took the family—when he took them at all—on his own terms.

That was fine with Rhys. He didn't feel like sharing the intimate details of his life either.

He met Nathan in Vancouver. They spent the week prowling the coastline of Vancouver Island, then renting a boat and a guide and checking out some of the smaller islands. They slept in bivy sacks on hard ground, ate food out of cans, and more than once got drenched from heavy rains.

Rhys loved it. Got distracted by it. And every time his thoughts drifted to Mariah it was easy to shove them away.

The week ended all too quickly. Nathan headed back to Paris where he lived when he wasn't off shooting photos somewhere.

Rhys headed back to New York.

But coming home didn't feel nearly as good as it usually did. Of course, he reminded himself, he wasn't coming home from weeks of firefighting. He was coming home from vacation.

To what?

A host of handsome hunks all slavering over Mariah?

No, thanks. So he stopped at a phone booth in the airport and called his brother, Dominic.

"Don't suppose you want to go fishing again?"

Dominic ran the family business, with interference from their father. He was consumed with work, trying to prove to the old man that he was perfectly capable, competent and could run things even better than the old man. It was true, but their father couldn't see that.

Rhys was wondering why he'd bothered when Dominic said, "Fishing? Hell, why not? Now?"

"If you want…"

"I'll pick you up at seven tomorrow morning. We can head out to Montauk again."

It made going home easier—knowing he'd be leaving in the morning. He spent the evening doing his laundry. He avoided his living room, avoided being able to see the stoop. Didn't want to see if Mariah was going up or down with the Hunk of the Week.

Didn't care!

He was up bright and early and was ready when Dominic came.

"We'll catch a ton," Dominic grinned when Rhys got in the car. "It'll be great."

"I'm surprised you were able to get away so easily."

His brother shrugged, keeping his eyes on the traffic. "Needed to. The old man has been coming around lately. Meddling."

"I thought he'd backed out of the day-to-day business stuff."

Another shrug. This one slightly more uncomfortable. "This isn't entirely business."

Rhys's eyebrows lifted. When had their father ever *not* been obsessed with business?

But Dominic didn't elaborate until they were on the Throg's Neck Bridge. Then he said, fingers tight on the steering wheel, "He's found another woman."

Rhys's eyebrows went even higher. *"Dad?"*

Their father, Douglas Wolfe, a widower for over twenty years, had never been known to have any women since the death of Rhys's mother when he was eight, let alone another one. "What do you mean, he's got a woman? What's he going to do with a woman? Does he want to marry her?"

Dominic shot him a hard look. "No, he doesn't want to marry her! He wants *me* to marry her!" He raked his fingers through his hair. "He's been hauling them in left, right and sideways lately. He wants me to get married. Again."

Not that Dominic had been married before.

He'd come close, though. He'd been engaged.

And jilted on his wedding day.

Twelve years ago, Dominic had been going to marry Carin Campbell, the daughter of one of his father's business associates. It was a match made, if not in heaven, at least on Wall Street—the union of the heir to D. Wolfe Enterprises and the daughter of the head of Campbell Limited.

Everybody in the world had been invited to the Wolfe

family home in the Bahamas to witness what even Douglas Wolfe smugly and cheerfully called "the merger."

Rhys had been best man, Nathan having gone off to Antarctica at the last minute because he'd been given a chance to shoot penguins or some such thing.

The two of them, he and Dominic, had stood on the veranda, where the wedding was to take place, and had waited—and waited—for Carin to appear.

She never had.

Later they learned she'd fled the island that morning.

She was gone.

No one knew where.

No one, as far as Rhys knew, had seen her since. Not even her apoplectic old man.

No one brought Carin's name up around Dominic. No one brought up marriage around Dominic.

He'd missed Rhys's wedding to Sarah the following year. He'd been in Hong Kong on business. Deliberately.

"Still touchy," Douglas had explained to Rhys. "He'll get over it."

But he'd never been willing to risk marriage again.

"He's trying to shove another girl down my throat," Dominic said wearily now. "He's getting frantic."

"Why?"

"He'll be seventy next month. Old as the hills, he says. One foot in the grave, to hear him tell it. 'The line is dying off,'" Dominic quoted in his best Douglas Wolfe imitation. He sighed. "He wants grandchildren."

Rhys looked away.

The old man would be over the moon if he found out about Mariah. He'd be dragging Rhys to the altar himself.

Rhys shut his eyes.

"The world isn't run by one irritating old man," Dominic growled.

"No," Rhys said.

They stared straight ahead, the two of them. To look back, to face the past, was to see the pain of failure, of hopes dashed, of dreams broken.

"I won't do it," Dominic said harshly.

"No," Rhys said again.

Neither would he.

They fished for five days. They went out in a boat every morning, they prowled the shoreline. When they returned in the evenings, they walked miles on the beach.

They didn't speak again about women or about their father. They talked about the weather and the fish. They argued about bait and about baseball. They caught a ton of fish.

It was wonderful. Elemental. As being with Nathan had been.

Rhys loved it. He felt strong. Powerful. In control.

He didn't even flinch when, as they drove back into the city, Dominic suggested he share some of his catch with his neighbor.

"The woman upstairs," Dominic said vaguely. "What's her name?"

"Mariah."

Dominic nodded. "Yeah, Mariah. She'd probably appreciate it."

Maybe she would. Maybe it would be a good thing to do.

He could stop in and give her some fish. Be friendly. Casual. Get things back on an even footing. Yeah, maybe he would.

He imagined himself going upstairs later that evening and knocking on her door. He'd hand her a big parcel of freshly caught flounder and tell her to enjoy it.

But when he went up later that night she wasn't there.

He scowled. He rocked on his heels. He held the damn packet of fish in his hands and fumed.

Mrs. Alvarez came up the steps. "You're back."

He nodded. "I just…stopped up to give Mariah some fish."

"She's out." Mrs. Alvarez smiled. "With Kevin."

Rhys's eyebrows drew down. *Who the hell was Kevin?*

"You give it to her tomorrow. She'll be in late tonight," Mrs. Alvarez suggested.

"How late?"

Mrs. Alvarez shrugged happily. "Dunno. But you're always out late when you're having a good time."

Rhys stood there, glowering, as she trundled past and went on up the next flight of stairs. He glanced at his watch. It was almost ten.

That was late enough.

He stomped back down the steps and stuck the fish in the refrigerator. Then he picked up his address book and thumbed through it, feeling irritable and itchy and in the need to do something.

He knew plenty of women. One of them ought to be willing to do something on the spur of the moment.

Carrie? Annie? Shauna? Teresa?

Teresa, he decided, and punched in her number to see if she wanted to catch a late film. In the old days Mariah would have been willing.

"The old days are over," he reminded himself as he stabbed in the numbers.

Teresa was willing too. Delighted, in fact. Delighted to go to a film with him, eager, it seemed, to spend the night with him.

"You can come back here after. Stick around," she offered, running a hand up his arm, curving it around his neck and pulling his head down for a quick teasing kiss.

Rhys shifted away. "I'm pretty bushed," he told her, yawning. "Another time?"

She rubbed against him provocatively. "You bet your boots, sweetheart."

He noticed that Mariah's light was still on when he came in. It was almost one a.m.

Pregnant women needed their sleep. He was sure they did.

And tomorrow when he took her the fish he'd tell her so.

CHAPTER FIVE

"OH, IT'S you."

Mariah stood gripping the front door of her apartment at eight-thirty the next morning, bleary-eyed and rumpled in an oversized T-shirt and shorts, looking like death warmed over.

"Hard night?" Rhys drawled, annoyed all over again. He didn't know what time she'd come in, but by the time he'd gone to sleep at past two her light was still on upstairs.

Now she looked pale—ashen, almost—and not at all happy to see him.

Well, he wasn't exactly happy to see her either. Not like this.

"You look like hell," he told her bluntly.

"Thank you very much."

"It's the truth. And you wouldn't," he told her righteously, "if you got more rest. You shouldn't be up partying until all hours."

Her mouth opened. And shut.

"It can't be good for you, getting so little sleep," he went on. "Women like you need more rest."

"Women like me?" There was a hint of acid in her tone.

"Pregnant women." He said the words through his teeth. "You need your rest, Mariah. Obviously more than you're getting. You should be getting a good eight hours. And you shouldn't be out drinking and—"

"I wasn't out drinking!"

"—and you need good food, too. Here." He thrust the package of fresh fish at her. "Dom and I went fishing this week. We caught a ton. Take this. Have it for dinner. It's flounder. Lots of fatty acids. It's good for you.''

Her eyes went wide, her face stark white. She didn't say a word. She could have said thank you, he thought irritably. She could take the fish instead of standing there staring at it looking horrified.

Then she gagged, clapped her hand over her mouth and bolted away.

''What the hell—?'' Rhys, still clutching the packet of fish, went after her. The bathroom door slammed in his face. ''What are you—? Oh.''

And as he listened to the sound of retching beyond the door he caught a whiff of the fish in his hand.

Suddenly Mariah's pale face and bleary-eyed look took on another meaning.

''Oh, hell,'' he muttered. ''Oh, damn. I'll be right back,'' he told her through the door.

He didn't know if she heard him or not. He clattered down the stairs, stuffed the fish into his own refrigerator, washed his hands thoroughly if hastily, then hot-footed it back up to her apartment.

The door to the bathroom was still closed.

''Mariah?''

She didn't reply. Rhys paced the hallway outside it. How was he supposed to know she got sick in the mornings?

Was she sick *every morning*?

It was dead silent beyond the door.

He tapped. ''Mariah?'' he said a little more forcefully. ''Are you okay?''

Still nothing. Then at last he heard the water begin to run. He heard it splash. Then it shut off.

At last Mariah opened the door.

She still looked like death. He didn't say so this time. He started to reach out to steady her, then thought better of it. He jammed his hand in his pocket instead. "How are you doing? Okay now?" he said, willing her to say yes.

"Oh, fine." Her voice was raspy, her tone dry. "Just dandy. Can't you tell?" She gave him a disgusted look and padded past him toward her bedroom.

He went after her. "I didn't know. That you got sick. You can't think I brought the fish to make you sick."

She flopped down onto her bed and lay with her forearm covering her eyes as if he weren't even there.

Rhys rocked back on his heels, feeling awkward, helpless. "Can I...do anything?"

"Else?"

"Damn it, Mariah. I told you I didn't try to make you sick. What can I do for you?"

"I think you've done enough, Rhys." Her arm was still over her eyes.

He couldn't see her face. He needed to see her face. She scared him when she was like this.

He went over to the bed and sat down beside her. She rolled away. But he reached over and took her hand and pulled her arm away from her face. She tried to snatch it away, but he held her fast.

There was a bit of color in her cheeks again, though he guessed it was probably from anger, not from a return to good health. They stared at each other. She looked ragged, worn. No glow now, he thought.

"Can I bring you some water?"

"No."

"A soda, then? You ought to drink something." He wasn't sure why, but it seemed to make sense.

She hesitated, then sighed. "There's some ginger ale in the fridge."

"I'll get it."

"I don't need you doing me favors."

But he didn't pay any attention to her. He strode out of

the room and got the ginger ale, poured it into a glass and brought it back.

Mariah had pushed herself halfway up against the headboard of her bed. He handed her the glass and stood watching while she sipped.

"Stop staring," she muttered.

But he couldn't. It was the first time he'd seen her up close in ages. It was the first time he'd really looked at her in a long, long time. She looked fragile. It surprised him. Mariah had never seemed fragile in the least.

"I said, stop staring," she bit out.

"Sorry." This time he shifted his gaze. He paced around the small room. But there was nothing else to look at that interested him. Only her. He turned back. "Better?"

"Yes. Thanks." The last was grudging. She shoved herself farther up the headboard. "You don't have to wait around."

He ignored the invitation to leave. "Does this happen every day?"

"Only when I get handed packets of fish. Or corned beef and cabbage." At his blank look, she explained. "Sierra once brought some by for an early lunch. We had peanut butter and crackers instead."

"Want me to get you some crackers now?"

"I'm not...hungry."

"You have to eat." Besides fragile, she looked skinny. He couldn't ever remember thinking Mariah looked skinny before, either. "You're supposed to be gaining weight, aren't you? Not losing it."

"I'm not losing. Not anymore."

"You did?"

She shrugged. "At first. Some women lose weight at first. If they get sick."

"Have you been sick a lot?" He couldn't seem to stop asking questions.

"Some days. The doctor offered me some medication for it, but I don't like taking stuff. Not any more than I have to. And mostly I can live with it. It's getting better. Especially if I start the day a little slower and a little later than I used to."

"You used to get up early." He felt a pang of guilt. "I thought you'd like some fish," he muttered. He didn't let himself think about how determined he'd been to get here bright and early and make sure she regretted her late night.

Where the hell had she been?

The question was almost out of his mouth before he managed to squelch it. It wasn't his business where she'd been. And he didn't care.

"Thanks for the thought." She didn't sound sarcastic. She set the ginger ale down on the bedside table while he rocked from heels to toes and back again. She looked up at him. "You don't have to stand around, Rhys. I'm not going to perish. It's just morning sickness." She said the words bluntly.

"I know what it is," he retorted harshly. Sarah had had it, too. He'd brought her crackers and soda. He'd doted. He'd hovered.

The phone rang. Mariah picked it up. "Oh, Kevin! Hi. Just getting up." She yawned. "I know. I enjoyed it, too. This afternoon?" She paused, flipped through a planner beside her bed, then said, "Yes, that'd be great. See you then. Bye."

Rhys heard the smile in her voice when she said goodbye to Kevin Whoever-He-Was. He remembered that smile. She used to use it with him.

"One of your men?" he asked acidly, all sympathy evaporating.

"What? Oh, yes. I guess you could say that." Mariah did smile then, but the smile still seemed to be for Kevin.

"Think you're going to be well enough for him this afternoon?" Rhys couldn't seem to stop himself from asking.

Mariah nodded slowly. "I think so." Then, "Yes, I'm sure I will be."

He scowled at her. "I'll leave you to it, then. Maybe when he gets here you'll feel well enough to come down and get your fish."

He probably banged the door louder than he should have on the way out.

Kevin would laugh when she told him.

Kevin Maguire was The Office Stud—the Man of the Hour, the Flavor of the Month—the guy all the women in the building lusted after.

Kevin was her colleague whom she'd never, ever dated because he went through women the way Sierra went through hair color. Kevin was the man she'd spent until three in the morning with trying to put together a story last night. Kevin was the least likely guy in the universe to want to date a pregnant lady.

Which was why Mariah was surprised that afternoon when she told him that she'd used him as a defense mechanism, and Kevin said, "Why not? What are you doing tonight? Let's go out."

She couldn't imagine why he was asking her out now, and said so.

A wide grin slashed his handsome face. "I've never been out with a pregnant lady before."

"I'm a novelty."

"And a defense mechanism, too. Every other woman in New York I take out has marriage on her mind. You don't—at least not with me." He cocked his head. "So, how about it?"

Mariah had always liked Kevin—from a distance. She'd enjoyed working with him. And she thought dinner with him would very likely be preferable to dinner with the men in her sister Sierra's little black book. "Why not?" she said.

Afterwards she had second, third and fourth thoughts about agreeing, but just as she was about to change her mind she looked out her window and saw Rhys and some blonde bombshell in a bikini out in his back garden.

"Mr. Maguire, here I come," she said.

In fact, she and Kevin had a good time. He took her to a small, lively southwestern restaurant on the East Side and they talked shop and sports.

For all his incredible good looks and charm, Kevin was easy to be with. Mariah enjoyed herself, and when he brought her back home and said, "Want to do that again?" she agreed at once.

"How about tomorrow?"

And she agreed to that, too. After all, what did she have to stay home for?

"I had a good time tonight," he told her outside her front door. He touched her cheek, and she wondered fleetingly if he might kiss her, and wondered, too, what she'd do if he did. He hadn't made a single move on her all night.

Then he grinned and gave her a wink. "G'night, Mariah."

"Goodnight, Kev."

The next night they went to a dinner and a jazz club. Two nights after that they went to a film in Tribeca. The following week they went for a walk in the park and swing dancing in the pavilion outside of Lincoln Center.

Every unmarried woman in the office was amazed. Kevin, who reputedly dated women once or twice, then dropped them, was sticking like flypaper to Mariah.

"What have you got that we haven't?" they asked her.

A baby, Mariah was tempted to say.

But she didn't think it was an answer they'd want to

hear. And by now she understood why Kevin was marriage shy.

"I've already got a girl," Kevin told her grimly that first night, "back home in Cincinnati. At least I will have if she ever comes to her senses. But she isn't ready to settle down. She wants us to see other people." His mouth twisted. "So I do. But when I see other women they all want to get serious and I don't, so I date 'em once or twice and move on. It's a pain, if you want to know the truth. As far as I'm concerned, you're a godsend."

That's me, Mariah thought, *patron saint of New York bachelors.*

But, as saviors went, Kevin did his part, too.

She had a man.

The multitudes had gone their way. She'd narrowed the field down to one. And she was seeing him a lot. Damn near every night of the week!

Rhys supposed he should be glad.

Hell, he *was* glad.

It was what he wanted, wasn't it? For Mariah to find a guy who would support her, who would be there for her? A man who would bring her crackers and soda, who would give her back rubs and go to Lamaze classes with her? A man who would someday go to PTA meetings and chaperone junior high school dances with her, who would teach the kid to drive and would be the one to worry when he or she didn't come home on time.

Of course that was what he wanted!

But he also wanted to know if this guy was up to it.

He was a good-looking stud, Rhys had to give him that. Black hair, lean, hard good looks. Muscular. Tall. Taller than Rhys by a couple of inches. Well, maybe only an inch and a half, Rhys corrected himself, standing up straighter.

He figured Mariah's guy was about his age. A casual

dresser. Rhys had never seen him in a suit. He usually came calling wearing shorts and a T-shirt or khakis and a blue or white dressshirt with the sleeves rolled up. No tie.

That didn't sound very corporate.

Dominic always wore suits and ties. When he'd worked in his father's corporation Rhys had worn suits and ties. Was this guy some dropout? He wasn't a freeloader, was he? Some gigolo who was going to take advantage of a defenseless woman? What if he didn't even have a job?

How was he going to find out?

He called his brother, Dominic. "When you want to scope out somebody, what do you do?"

"A competitor, you mean?" Dominic asked.

"Yes. I mean, no." Rhys scratched the back of his head. "Hell, I don't know. I want to know about some guy. Who he is. What he does for a living. If he's trustworthy."

There was a pause on the other end of the line. Rhys could hear Dominic's unspoken, *Why?*

"What's his name?" Dominic asked instead.

"Kevin."

"Kevin what?"

"I don't know. I'll—I'll find out." *How the hell was he going to find out?*

"Are you okay, bro?" Dominic asked him.

"I'm fine," Rhys snapped. "I'm just…doing a favor for a friend. Checking someone out."

"Right," Dominic said. He was clearly unconvinced. "Get me his last name. I'll check him out."

Trouble was, Rhys didn't know how he was going to do that. He didn't have a lot of time. In fact, he was due to go back to work the day after tomorrow. He'd be a lot happier going if he knew Mariah's guy was up to snuff.

He scowled. He prowled. He paced.

He debated calling Sierra and asking just who this Kevin guy was. Then he remembered his close encounter with her

Doc Martens and changed his mind. He debated calling
Izzy or Chloe. He rejected that idea, too. Izzy had glared
at him in the grocery store last week. Normally voluble,
she had barely said a word. He'd seen Chloe in Zabar's.
She'd looked askance and said, "Rhys, how could you?"

He didn't have to wonder anymore. Everyone knew.

He thought of trying to explain. He knew he wouldn't.
It wasn't any of their business. It was his—and Mariah's.
And no one else's.

So he couldn't ask them. Or Gib or Finn.

There was only one person he dared ask.

Mariah herself.

Yes, he'd ask Mariah. Confront her. Express his con-
cerns. The more he thought about it, the smarter it sounded.
It was the sane, responsible, adult thing to do.

So he waited until Kevin brought her home one night—
past midnight, Rhys thought irritably. And once he heard
Kevin leave, Rhys tucked in his shirt, combed his hair, and
went up to Mariah's flat.

It opened almost at once. "Forget someth—? Oh." Her
tone changed and her smile faded. "What do you want?"

"I want to know his name."

She blinked. "What? Whose name?"

Rhys jerked his head toward the stairs down which Kevin
had recently departed. "Your stud."

Mariah's eyes went wide. Color rose in her cheeks. "I
beg your pardon?" she said with enough ice to sink the
Titanic.

"You heard me. What's his name? Loverboy? Is he re-
liable? Trustworthy? Does he have a job? He's over here
day and night!" He hadn't meant to be accusing. He'd
intended to simply ask a few questions, get a few answers.

"Go to hell, Rhys." She started to close the door.

He stuck his foot in it. "Just wait a damn minute!"

"No, you wait! How dare you? What do you think

you're doing, barging in here asking me questions about something that's none of your business?''

"As your friend—"

"*Friend?*" She snorted.

Rhys felt heat begin to burn in his face. "Friend," he insisted. "Just because—"

"I'm pregnant with your child and you want nothing to do with either of us, and you still think you're my friend?" She was incredulous.

"I want what's best for you."

"Of course you do." Not. He could see it in her eyes.

"I don't want to see you taken advantage—"

"Buzz off, Rhys. Get out of here. Like I said, just go to hell!" She gave the door another hard shove, and kept shoving. Her face was red from exertion. She was going to hurt herself pushing like that.

He sighed and pulled his foot out. The door slammed in his face.

He stared at it. "Fine," he said much more mildly than he felt like saying it. "Go ahead. Marry him. Whatever." Then he turned and stomped back down the stairs.

"Marry him"? "Whatever"?

Hours passed. Mariah replayed the scene all night. Ran it through, dissected it, picked it to pieces. By the next morning she still couldn't believe her ears.

One minute Rhys was barging in here wanting to know about Kevin, and the next he was stalking away telling her to marry him? It didn't make sense.

Rhys didn't make sense.

Nothing made sense.

"Maybe he cares," Sierra said. She had brought bagels this time. Mariah could eat bagels. She chewed on one thoughtfully. "Weird."

Mariah thought so, too. A month ago she would have

taken Rhys's interference for a sign that he did care. Now she wasn't sure what it was. Or what to hope it was.

She wasn't sure she ought to have hopes anymore.

"I really do know some good guys," Sierra said. "Just met one last week when I was working at a shoot in Central Park. He looks dishy in a G-string," she added with a grin.

Mariah tried to muster a smile. "Maybe not."

"Still got it bad for the jerk?" Sierra asked.

"I guess I do."

It was galling to admit it. She didn't want to give a damn. He didn't!

Did he?

It was a relief to leave.

The minute he headed to the airport, Rhys felt his heart lighten. He breathed deeper. More easily. Another few hundred miles and he'd have his equilibrium back. After he'd taught a week-long seminar in oil fire containment in Texas, he'd be himself again.

He was sure of it.

When Rhys was on the road, teaching or, even better, fighting a fire, nothing existed outside the moment. Nothing mattered but the present.

He never thought about anything else.

Or he never had until now.

Now, damn it, he caught sight of a pregnant woman on the plane and he couldn't help but think of Mariah. He saw copies of the magazine she wrote for in the airport terminal. The cover featured an article about bank CEO Sophia Leddington—one that found the warm and witty woman behind the suit. Rhys remembered when Mariah had done the interview.

She seemed to be following him, pursuing him wherever he went.

He bought a sports magazine and a news weekly and a

thick paperback thriller. They would keep him busy when he wasn't working.

They didn't keep him busy enough.

Baseball was only so distracting. Reading about tennis had never been his thing. The thriller wasn't very thrilling. And he'd had the misfortune to pick one in which the missing woman was expecting a child.

When the hell had the world become so preoccupied with pregnant women?

He rented a car and drove out to South Padre Island when the work day was over. But that felt too much like being on vacation. And vacations to him still meant spending time with Mariah.

He wondered if she was still getting sick in the mornings.

He wondered if Kevin Whoever was still there every night.

He was glad when the week was over and he could move on to the next seminar. But Santa Barbara was no more distracting than Houston had been.

He wondered if he'd shut off the water in the sink.

Of course he had! He wouldn't have just gone off and left the water running! He was a smart guy, savvy, sensible. He left home all the time without doing dumb stuff. He wouldn't have forgotten to shut off the cold water tap.

Would he?

He supposed he could call Mariah and have her go down and check.

Oh, yeah. Sure. Just call her up and say, By the way, I might've left the water running ten days ago.

But if he didn't call her—and he had left it running—he'd be paying his water bill for the rest of his life.

You shut it off! he told himself.

But the niggling sense of worry didn't go away. He couldn't be sure.

Not unless he called and asked Mariah to check.

He called Mariah.

She sounded surprised to hear his voice. "Rhys? Why are you calling? What's wrong?"

"Nothing," he said brusquely, feeling foolish at once. "I just...was having a little trouble with the kitchen faucet. The plumber was supposed to come fix it. I wondered if you would mind going down and checking to see if it's okay now. That...the water's off."

"I didn't see a plumber," she said.

"You spend every minute watching my front door?"

"Of course not! I just...all right, fine. I'll go check."

"Take your time. I'll call you back." He gave her ten minutes. Long enough, he figured, for her to go down to his place and come back. And then, when he called her back, he could sort of casually find out how she was.

"Doesn't look like there's been a plumber there," she said when he called her back. "I didn't see anything new."

"He was just going to change the washer. It isn't cosmetic." Rhys dismissed the whole issue. "Thanks for doing it. How...how are you?"

"Me?" She sounded amazed that he would ask. "Fine."

"Are you still getting sick?"

"No."

"Feeling better, huh?" Oh, this was a terrific conversation. Really scintillating.

"Much."

Dead air. Then Rhys said heartily, "Well, glad to hear it. Thanks again. Bye." And he rang off.

God, he was an idiot! Why the hell had he bothered to call? What difference did it make?

None. Absolutely none.

But, oddly, he slept better that night.

The baby was getting bigger.

At four months, Mariah couldn't wear her regular jeans

and shorts anymore, not even with the zips pulled down. She spread her hands across her rapidly expanding abdomen and wondered what was going on. It seemed to her that, at this stage, Chloe hadn't been nearly this big.

And when she had dinner with Chloe and Gibson the following Friday Chloe confirmed it. Due to deliver any day, Chloe was presently somewhat the same size as a bus and she couldn't seem to find a comfortable position in her chair.

"I didn't need maternity clothes until I was past four months," she said, then looked down at her belly and sighed. "Seems hard to believe," she said, "that I was ever as slim as you." She looked at Mariah's still relatively small tummy enviously. "Ah, well. Won't be long." She patted her abdomen. "Ready to go, kiddo?" she asked her unborn child.

"Not now," Gibson said quickly. "We haven't eaten yet."

"I'm not supposed to eat if I'm going into labor," Chloe informed him.

He looked stricken. "Are you?" He was half out of his chair, looking at his wife with a mixture of concern and alarm.

"No." Chloe smiled beatifically. She put her hand over his and squeezed gently. "I'll let you know in plenty of time."

Gibson took a shaken, nervous breath and settled back down. He gave Mariah a wry look as he picked up his beer. "She knows I'm going to panic when the time comes. She thinks it's funny."

Mariah grinned. It was funny. And touching. Watching them together was always funny and touching.

It always gave her a lump in her throat to watch Gibson and Chloe or Finn and Izzy together. Both couples were so in love, so in tune with each other. Finn and Gibson were both hard-driving, intense men, as alike in temperament as men could be. Their wives were very different—Izzy a little dizzy and Chloe gentle and practical. And yet both marriages worked.

Because they loved each other.

Mariah envied them that love. She envied them that their love was reciprocated. She smiled a little wistfully.

She went home and thought of Rhys. She shouldn't. It didn't do her any good. He hadn't called back. She didn't even know why he'd called in the first place. All that nonsense about a plumber! Had he been checking up on her?

And if he had, what did it mean?

The phone ringing woke her.

She sat up, panicked, and, in the early morning light, groped for the telephone. "What?" she demanded. The clock on the bedside table said 5:47.

"It's a boy!" Gib crowed.

All the air seemed to whoosh right out of her. Mariah sagged back against the pillows, dazed and relieved.

"Did you hear me?" Gib could have been heard in Albany. "Seven pounds thirteen ounces. Twenty-one inches long. Blond hair—what there is of it. And Chloe's eyes. Swear to God, Mariah, he's got violet-blue eyes!"

Mariah smiled. She laughed softly. "The girls will be drooling over him."

Gib laughed, too, and it sounded suspiciously like he'd been crying. "All in good time," he said. "He's got a little growing up to do first."

"Not much. I'll be up to see him later today. I expect to do my share of drooling. How's Chloe?"

"Good." He breathed a sigh of relief. "Remarkable. She was a trouper. God, I almost died just watching. And she never batted an eye. Acted like having babies was a picnic."

Mariah kept right on smiling as she listened to the doting husband, the proud father. She doubted Chloe had thought it was a picnic. She bet Chloe had batted her eyes more than once or twice. She had no doubt, though, that Chloe had been a trouper. She was just glad Gib noticed.

Of course he'd noticed. He loved Chloe. Desperately. Mariah had never seen a man as shattered as Gib had been last year when Chloe had gone back to Iowa and he'd thought she was going to marry Dave.

He'd been a wreck then. He was a wreck again now. A good wreck. A happy wreck.

"They're beautiful," he told Mariah now. "Both of 'em."

"I know." Mariah was sure of it. "I'll be up to see you all later." Then she settled back down in her bed and added softly, "Congratulations, Gib."

She reached out and set the receiver on the cradle, then dragged the extra pillow tight beneath the quilt and hard against her abdomen, liking the feel of it there, warm and supporting. Other women had their husbands' backs to hug.

Mariah hugged a pillow.

She swallowed hard and blinked back sudden dampness in her eyes. It was just that she was happy for Gib and Chloe and their brand-new son.

It had nothing to do with her own life.

She could make it with a pillow. Other women did.

Other single parents got by every day of the week. So could she.

"We're going to make it just fine," she whispered to the baby now. "You and me, we're a team. And everything's going to be fine. Got that?" She reached between the pillow and her belly and gave it a gentle rub.

And felt an odd fluttering under her fingers.

She jerked. "What?" She pressed her fingers hard against her abdomen.

And felt it again. Fluttering!

"Oh, my God!" She sat straight up, threw back the covers and stared at her belly. She flattened both hands against her stomach and sat completely still. Waited.

And there it was again!

Like butterfly wings inside her. She laughed. And felt lighter. Happier. Stronger. No longer one against the world.

They *were* a team. There would be the two of them.

Even though nothing had changed, everything was different.

It came again. Here. No, there. Boy, could that baby move!

She hugged the pillow to her as another half laugh, half sob welled up inside her.

"Ah, Rhys," she whispered. "You don't know what you're missing."

She went to the hospital that afternoon.

She was looking forward to going, to meeting this new person. Brendan Gibson Walker. All seven pounds thirteen ounces of him.

She found him asleep in a bassinet in Chloe's room, one fist in his mouth, butt in the air. While the proud mother and father looked on, Mariah bent and studied him. She couldn't see the color of his eyes, but he had fair hair like his mother and his father's nose. She thought she could see the best of both in this beautiful child.

"He's lovely," she said softly. "Gorgeous."

"Gib's already taken half a dozen rolls of film." Chloe laughed.

"What's the use of having a camera if you aren't going to use it?" Gib said practically. He winked at Mariah, then looked at his wife with an expression that was such a combination of love and tenderness that Mariah felt another tug of longing for a relationship like theirs.

She thought of Rhys who perhaps once had felt that way about another woman. And she couldn't help wishing he felt that way about her. Her throat felt tight and achy and she swallowed hard. This wasn't the time to indulge herself in hopeless wishes. It was a time to rejoice—to take part in the joy that Gib and Chloe so obviously shared.

Just then Brendan opened his eyes, blinked and yawned around his fist. And Mariah could see that his eyes really were a deep blue-violet.

"Oh, my," she said. "You will have to fight the girls off this one."

"Terrifying, isn't it?" Chloe agreed cheerfully as Brendan began to root around in his bassinet, apparently looking for his next meal. "Bring him to me, will you?"

"Me?" Mariah looked at her, startled.

"Do you mind? I just thought you might want to get a head start on what you're going to be doing before too long." She gave Mariah a conspiratorial smile.

"Oh. Right." Nervously, Mariah scooped Brendan up into her arms. He was so…tiny. So fragile. So helpless. She felt a momentary sense of panic. How was she going to cope with someone just like him depending on her?

She touched his hand and automatically Brendan's tiny fingers locked around one of hers. His grip was amazingly strong. He whimpered and nuzzled and looked up at her through curious, unfocussed eyes. "Just a minute, buddy," she told him, and carried him to Chloe and settled him in his mother's arms.

Brendan found her breast at once and glommed on. Mariah, watching, felt her body respond, as if there was some inner connection between her, an expectant mother, and this other mother and child.

It was odd. Primal. She wondered at it even as she felt that new flutter in her abdomen again. Her murmur of surprise had Gib and Chloe looking her way.

"Kicking you already, is he?" Chloe asked. She fixed Brendan with a loving glare. "He did his share."

"Not really kicking yet," Mariah said. "Unless maybe it's flutter kicks. Still got room to maneuver, I guess. Sure feels like it." Her hand traced the pattern of the flutter, moving here and there.

"Fast swimmer," Gib said with a grin. "I was amazed the first time I felt Brendan move." He shook his head at the memory. "It was the first time it seemed like he was real."

"To you. You weren't the one throwing up and growing out of your clothes," Chloe reminded him.

They smiled at each other again.

Mariah stayed a few minutes longer. Then she said she had to go. "I have a doctor's appointment. Just a monthly check. He's going to do an ultrasound today."

"So you'll get to see your swimmer," Gib said.

Mariah hadn't thought about that. It made her smile. She left them a few minutes later, and they were still smiling— at her, at their son, at each other. At the world.

Rhys had never been happy to fight a fire before.

He welcomed the distraction now. He didn't care that he'd been called out of bed in Santa Barbara in the middle of the night and sent to Alaska. It was fine with him.

He focused on what needed to be done the moment he got there. It took all his skill, all his energy, everything he had.

But he couldn't fight the fire every waking moment. And he couldn't control the content of his dreams.

And that was where Mariah seemed to blindside him.

It made him twitchy and irritable. It made him short-tempered and sharp. He was annoyed with himself for not being able to forget her.

He wanted to forget her! He needed to forget her!

The trouble was, he couldn't.

It's because she isn't settled, he told himself. If he knew she was being taken care of, he'd be off the hook. If he were sure that ol' Kevin Whoever was capable of being her husband and a father, Rhys assured himself that everything would be fine.

She would be fine. He would be fine. The baby would be fine.

But he didn't know.

He needed to find out.

One more phone call wouldn't hurt. Even though he'd never called her from work before this time out, things needed to be settled. It wasn't as if he was calling her every day.

He checked his watch. It was four p.m. in New York. A good time to get hold of her—well after any lingering sickness she might be feeling and, hopefully, before Kevin Whoever turned up for the evening.

He punched in her number before he could think twice about it. The phone rang. And rang. He got her answering machine and stood there frozen, completely unprepared to leave a message.

Then the phone picked up. "Hello?" she said. Her voice was breathy, gasping, as if she'd run.

"It's Rhys," he said briskly. "Did you just come in?"

"I…yes. I…" And then she didn't say anything at all.

He waited. Got nothing. "Mariah? Are you okay?"

"I'm…fine."

Swell. They were going to have another useless conversation.

But then she said, "I felt 'em moving, Rhys." There was excitement in her voice. "I went to the doctor today. I saw them on the ultrasound." There was more excitement in her tone now. Also amazement. Astonishment.

And Rhys, repeating the words in his head, felt a quickening sense of panic. "What did you say? You saw *them* moving?"

She gave a giddy, slightly hysterical laugh. "Yes! It's twins!"

CHAPTER SIX

TWINS?

Rhys was stunned. Pole-axed. Appalled.

He'd called her up just to make sure Kevin Whatever-His-Name was capable of parenting one kid.

And now she was having *two*?

Cripes. Rhys took a deep breath. And then another. It didn't seem to be doing a lot of good. He felt light-headed, desperate for air.

Two? It boggled the mind.

God, he wondered desperately, what were You thinking? His thoughts were prayer. Supplication. Pure panic.

"How do you know?' he demanded hoarsely when he could finally speak.

"I told you! I saw them!"

"What?"

"In the ultrasound. It was just amazing. There they were!" She sounded breathy, excited, and still a little disbelieving herself. "Moving around. Floating. Swimming, you know?"

He didn't know. Couldn't imagine. Was trying to. He opened his mouth, then shut it again, having no idea whatsoever what he should say.

"I didn't realize what I was seeing at first," Mariah said. "The doctor had to tell me. But then I could see. There were *two of them*! It was amazing. Just amazing. Rhys?" she said when he didn't reply.

"Huh?" He managed that much. He couldn't manage more. He looked around for someplace to sit down.

"Rhys, aren't you...? Don't you...? No, of course you

don't.'' The eager breathiness left her voice. It was flat
now, colorless. Then she murmured, "I wish…" But she
didn't finish that thought.

Rhys wished he'd never called. "Are you…going to
be…all right?"

"Of course I'll be all right." She sounded brisk and dis-
missive now.

"You're sure? You…feel okay?"

"I feel fine." There was annoyance in her voice.

"Well, good. Good," he repeated with more enthusiasm.
"Glad to hear it."

"What did you want?"

"What? Oh, not much." He couldn't ask if Kevin was
equipped to handle a baby now—not when they weren't
talking about one single baby anymore! Who the hell was
ever equipped to handle twins? "I just had a break. I'm in
Alaska, got here three days ago. Things are pretty much
under control now, and I…well, I just thought I'd give you
a call."

She didn't say anything to that.

So he forced himself to go on. "You're watering my
garden, aren't you?" In times past, it had always been understood that she would.

"I'm watering your tomatoes, Rhys." Her voice was flat.

There was another long pause. A *pregnant* pause, Rhys
thought savagely. Two of them? She was having twins? He
still couldn't imagine.

Then Mariah said, "There's someone knocking at the
door. I have to go."

Kevin? Rhys wondered. He didn't feel as if he could ask.

"Right. I'll let you go, then." Twins. He exhaled with a
shake of the head. "Take care of yourself, Mariah."

"Yes," she said.

And she was gone.

Slowly Rhys put the receiver back on the cradle, then

just stood there, unmoving. He tried to think about what she'd told him, tried to make it real. He couldn't.

Mariah was going to have two babies? He, who wanted no ties, no strings, no responsibilities, no commitments, was about to become the father of twins?

No.

He stared at the phone. Maybe he hadn't really picked it up and called her. Maybe he'd just dreamed the whole thing.

He could hope.

He hoped.

For three more weeks, he hoped. And worried and fumed. He and his crew finished up in Alaska. They got sent to Venezuela. He usually never minded where they went or how long they were gone. It had never mattered to him before.

It did now. He was antsy. Irritated. Worried.

And he didn't want to worry. Damn it, caring—and worrying—was exactly what he didn't want to do!

He wanted to go home, to sort things out. To make sure things were taken care of—to make sure *Mariah* was taken care of. If he could do that, things would be all right. *He* would be all right.

His boss wanted to send him to the North Sea after Venezuela.

For the first time in his career, he said no.

He went home.

He got in first thing in the morning. He'd flown all night. He felt like something scraped up off the bottom of a bird cage. He needed, as he always did, a shower, a cold beer and about ten hours' sleep.

But first he went up to see Mariah.

She looked astonished when she opened the door and found him standing there.

He was astonished, too—at how much she'd changed—
grown!—since he'd been gone. She looked as if she had a
beach ball shoved under her baggy T-shirt. The rest of her,
though, was skin and bones.

"My God, don't you eat?" he demanded.

"What? Of course I— Where do you think you're going?" She grabbed his arm as he stalked straight into her
apartment, right through the living room and into the
kitchen. He jerked open the refrigerator. She had cheese,
eggs, celery, green peppers, yogurt. Rabbit food, he
thought, disgusted.

"You're not getting sick anymore, are you?"

"No, but—"

"Fine. I'll go get us some steak and be right back." He
headed for the door.

"Rhys!" She came after him. "It's nine-thirty in the
morning! What do you think you're doing? You can't barge
in here and just…just…"

He looked back over his shoulder. "I just did," he told
her mildly. "And I don't give a damn what time it is. I'll
be back. Got any potatoes?"

"No, I—"

"I'll bring some of them, too."

He went to the grocery on Broadway and got the steak
and the potatoes. He bought beer, too. He was back within
the hour. He didn't bother to go to his place to shave and
shower. She could take him the way he was.

She was slow opening the door when he knocked, and
he wondered if she wasn't going to respond. He was just
considering his alternatives, when she finally did.

"This isn't necessary," she said as he brushed past her
with the grocery bag and headed for the kitchen.

"Looks to me like it is," he said. He knew his way
around her kitchen. He got out a frying pan and a pot to

boil the potatoes in. ''Set the table,'' he said over his shoulder.

''I had breakfast.''

''And I haven't. Humor me.'' He said it through his teeth and gave her a look that set her to doing what he asked.

''Bully,'' she muttered as she slapped plates on the table.

''Somebody's got to, apparently.''

''I thought you didn't want any part of me—or the baby…babies,'' she corrected herself.

I don't! But he didn't say that. He peeled the potatoes and cubed them as the water started to boil. He focused on preparing the meal. He didn't look at Mariah. Not straight on. Not intently. It seemed too personal, too intimate.

He'd made love with her—and now he couldn't look at her body—at the changes his lovemaking had wrought. Even thinking about it annoyed him. He poked at the steak as it cooked.

Mariah, who had finished setting the table, stood watching him. He could feel her gaze on his back. He wanted to turn around, wanted to look at her, to see the woman who was his friend, to smile at her. To have everything that had happened between them go away.

But it wouldn't.

So he would do this.

He would take care of her. For now. He would see that she got square meals. That she survived this pregnancy.

And then…?

That was someplace he wouldn't go.

She couldn't figure him out.

He was grouchy, pushy, bossy and controlling—and all the while he made it quite clear he wished he didn't have to be there at all.

''Go away,'' she told him.

She must have told him ten times that first morning when

he'd pushed his way into her apartment. He'd been grubby and rumpled, his hair mussed, his cheeks unshaven, his eyes bloodshot. "Go home," she'd said.

She'd told him the same thing a dozen times since. He never listened. He never answered. He never smiled. Or talked.

Worst of all, he never left.

He seemed to think she couldn't cope without him.

"I don't need you!" she told him after his third day of appearing on the dot of six to cook her dinner.

"You need someone," he said implacably, heading toward the kitchen. "Where's What's-His-Face?"

Mariah, frowning, followed him. "What's-Whose-Face?"

"Kevin." He spat the name as if it were a swear word.

"He's in Cincinnati this week."

Kevin's girl had had a change of heart. At least he hoped she had. He'd taken a week's vacation and had gone home to test the waters.

'Figures," Rhys snorted. "Threw you over, did he? Two kids too many for him?"

"What?" Then she said quite honestly, "We haven't discussed it."

"You need to."

"Why? So you can be off the hook?"

He opened his mouth, and closed it again. "You can't do this alone," was all he said.

Mrs. Alvarez smiled at him.

A lot.

She nodded approvingly every time she saw him going up the stairs to Mariah's apartment. She beamed when she saw the two of them together. She gave Mariah thumb's-up signs.

Mariah didn't respond.

She didn't seem all that thrilled that he was busting his butt trying to help her. She acted as if it was some big imposition. She kept telling him it wasn't necessary. He got the feeling she wanted to be rid of him.

Well, there was nothing he'd like better than to be gone, damn it. Just as soon as some other guy stepped into the breach...

And then one afternoon he rang up to tell her he'd take her out to dinner tonight instead of cooking for her, and some guy answered the phone.

"Who's calling?" he asked.

"Who the hell wants to know?" Rhys snapped back.

There was a second's pause. Then the guy said, "This is Kevin Maguire. And you are—?"

There was a far longer pause before Rhys bit out, "Rhys Wolfe. Tell Mariah I'll pick her up for dinner at six-thirty."

And Kevin Maguire, damn his arrogant hide, said, "Oh, that won't be necessary. Mariah said if you called to tell you she and I are going out."

"Out?" Rhys sputtered.

But all he got was a dial tone.

How dared she? She was supposed to be eating with him! At least, he'd assumed she'd be eating with him. They'd eaten together ever since he'd come back. And yes, she'd told him Kevin was only gone for a week, but that didn't mean...

Apparently it did mean...

"Well, fine," he muttered. "Good." Let ol' Kevin have her. Let's just see if he wants her, Rhys thought with a certain grim satisfaction.

He didn't call her that night. He watched through the curtain as she went out with Kevin. Kevin was holding her arm as they came down the steps and moved down the sidewalk.

Rhys glowered after them as he watched them go.

Mariah seemed to sway when she walked, as if she hadn't quite figured out how to balance the load yet.

The load. The *babies*.

His babies.

His fingers knotted into fists in the pockets of his jeans. He didn't want to think about that.

He waited up to see if she would call him. If Kevin threw her over, he supposed the least he could do was stay awake for it.

She didn't call.

He heard her come in. It was close to midnight, and it made him gnash his teeth that she'd stayed out so late. And he waited up a good hour after he made sure Kevin Maguire had gone again, but she never rang.

Maybe she was waiting for morning.

She didn't call in the morning, either.

Finally, he called her. "What'd he say?" he asked without preamble.

"I beg your pardon?"

"Don't play games, Mariah. What'd Loverboy say about the...twins?"

"He thinks two is a lovely number."

Rhys's eyes narrowed. His fingers tightened on the telephone. "It didn't scare him off?"

"Were you hoping it had?"

"No!"

There was a long silence. "Then I guess you're in luck," Mariah said quietly.

Rhys heard the receiver click in his ear.

"I'll come around as much as you want," Kevin said glumly as he sat with his elbows propped on Mariah's kitchen table, his head in his hands. "What the hell else have I got to do?"

His girlfriend was still dithering. She was "almost sure"

he was the guy for her. She just needed "a little more time."

Mariah patted his shoulder as she passed. "She'll come around." A platitude if ever there was one, and she was sure Kevin knew it. After all, look who was talking!

Rhys certainly hadn't come around—except physically. And that was somehow worse than his not being there at all.

"I don't mean to take advantage," she said.

"Misery loves company," Kevin told her.

They were two of the most loving people in New York. They spent almost every evening together. Mariah took to dropping by the office to write instead of doing it at home, ostensibly because she was getting claustrophobic staring at her apartment walls all day. In fact, she didn't want to be there when Rhys was.

Because then she wanted Rhys.

And didn't want him at the same time.

She felt as if her brain was as scrambled as her emotions. The August heat didn't help.

They called it "the dog days of summer"—those ghastly few days when the humidity made people wish they'd been born with gills, and the heat, especially in the city, was like a blanket, suffocating them all. Any self-respecting dog, Mariah was convinced, would never be caught dead outside in weather like this.

It was over a hundred for the fourth day in a row, and as she dragged herself home that afternoon Mariah almost regretted having agreed to go to Mooney Vaughan's rehearsal at Carnegie Hall that morning.

Vaughan, one of America's most famous jazz trombonists, had told her they could meet the next afternoon. But Mariah had known that Kevin was going to be busy all day today squiring some potential advertisers around the city.

She didn't want to be sitting home alone.

So she'd said she'd go to the rehearsal, then have lunch and the afternoon with Mooney, talking about his life and work for her next article.

It was the perfect solution. She wouldn't have to worry about running into Rhys.

And it worked—until she dragged her way home late that afternoon. There had been a terrific traffic jam and the bus she'd been on had lost its air-conditioning. Finally she'd got out and walked. And walked. And walked.

She tried to get a cab, but there never seemed to be any cabs at five o'clock—except off-duty ones. Certainly she didn't see one that wanted to stop for her.

So she walked slowly, took her time, and still nearly died by the time she got home. She sat down on the stoop, unwilling to tackle the stairs until she felt as if she wouldn't die en route.

The ornamental gate below the stoop opened. "Hey," Rhys said.

He looked cool—and rested—and beautiful. And Mariah, who felt hot and exhausted and like something normally found on the curb, hated him. She looked at him, then turned away and shut her eyes. She did not have the strength to deal with him.

He came out through the wrought-iron gate and peered down at her. "Are you okay?"

Mariah didn't open her eyes. She stretched out on the steps and let as much of the breeze created by people walking past reach her over-heated skin. "Just peachy."

A cool hand on her cheek startled her into opening her eyes. "What are you—?"

He grabbed her hand and began hauling her to her feet. "Come on."

"What? Where are you—?"

But it was perfectly clear where he was taking her— down the steps and into his place.

"Rhys!" she protested, but to no avail. And once he had his door open and she was hit with the blessed coolness of his air-conditioned apartment she stopped arguing.

She would stay a minute. Just a minute. She would catch her breath. And then—

"Sit down." He sat her on the sofa, lifted her feet onto the coffee table in front of it, then dropped her bag with her tape recorder and notebooks on the floor beside her. "Water? Iced tea? Juice?"

"Water," she said. "Please," she added, contriving not to sound like someone gasping their way to an oasis.

Thirty seconds later he was back and pressing a glass of water with ice cubes into her hand.

He thought she looked as if she was going to faint. He'd just happened to be standing by the window when he'd seen her come up the street. Even three houses away he could tell her face was abnormally flushed, and she wasn't moving with her typically brisk stride. At first he'd assumed it was because she was carrying a lot of baby. Then he'd decided it was more than that. Especially when she'd sagged on the stoop.

He'd practically shot out the door. He'd had to stop and school himself to sound casual.

"Don't gulp," he said now.

"You are so bossy," she complained. "You didn't used to be this bossy."

"You didn't used to need telling what to do."

"I don't—" she began to argue.

He spread his hands. "Okay. Fine. You're coping. You're doing swell. But people are dropping like flies all over the city. Have you been listening to the radio? Two hundred and forty-seven cases of heatstroke just this afternoon. Two hundred and forty-eight, judging from the looks of you."

"I don't have heatstroke," she protested. She'd finished the water and was looking at the glass longingly.

"I'll get you some more. Stay there." A glower fixed her where she sat. He brought her another glass. She drank this one more slowly. When she finished, she looked up and smiled. It was a pale imitation of a real Mariah Kelly smile.

"Thank you," she said. She started to get up.

He blocked her way. "You don't have to leave right now."

"I—"

"Or is Loverboy waiting?"

She blinked, then shrugged. "Kevin, you mean. He'll be along later." Maybe. He hadn't thought he would be able to get over tonight as he and Stella were going to be taking these people out. But she wasn't telling Rhys that. "I don't want to disturb you."

"You'll disturb me if you faint on the steps."

"I won't faint! I just—"

"Look," he said. "I made a lot of chili this afternoon. Eat it with me."

"Kevin—"

"Isn't here now. And you look hungry. You have to eat, Mariah. Besides, you don't want to climb those steps right now. You know you don't."

Still she hesitated. She didn't want to start hoping again, either. And, even when she told herself she wouldn't, every time Rhys was nice to her, she couldn't help it—the dreams she'd thought well buried rose like the phoenix to taunt her again.

"Chili, Mariah," he said. Tempting her. "Green salad. Tomatoes from the garden."

Damn it, she thought. *Stop being nice! I hate it when you're nice.*

"Chocolate ice cream for dessert."

God, he knew her weaknesses. She sighed. "Fine," she said ungraciously. "You win."

He grinned. "It'll be ready in a few minutes. Want something else to drink? Beer?"

"No. I...I'm not drinking any alcohol."

"Oh. Right." He glanced in the direction of her belly, then just as quickly away again. As if he couldn't bear to look.

Mariah glared at him.

"I'll get you some iced tea," he decided.

"Thank you," she said politely. *Keep it distant. Keep it impersonal,* she told herself. She folded her hands in her lap and smiled at him.

"You look like you're waiting for the dentist," Rhys muttered.

"What?"

He scowled. "Nothing. Just stay there. I'll get your tea."

He banged around the kitchen, almost dropped a glass, stirred the chili and fumed. How dared she sit there and act like some proper stranger?

You wanted something different? Rhys asked himself. Something *more*?

Well, no, but...

So it was just as well. She was a guest now.

He got out the pitcher of iced tea and poured a glass for her. Then he snagged a bottle of beer for himself.

He twisted the cap off and took a long swallow. A very long swallow. Then he stirred the chili again. Had he made so much because unconsciously he'd intended to ask her to dinner?

It wasn't a question he wanted to answer.

He took another swallow of the beer. Maybe he should have poured himself something stronger.

"Lemon, no sugar, right?" he called to her.

There was no reply. He didn't need one in any case. He

knew how Mariah drank her iced tea. He was just saying it to make conversation. *Polite* conversation. The kind they both wanted.

He picked up the glass and carried it back in.

She was asleep.

He stared. She was still on the sofa, but she no longer looked as if she was waiting for the dentist. She was nestled in it now, her arms curving loosely around her burgeoning middle, her head back, cheeks still flushed, her eyes closed. So much for the dentist.

He smiled. Couldn't help himself.

And he moved closer. Asleep, Mariah looked like a child. As if she was thirteen, not thirty. Or twenty-nine or however the hell old she was. She looked young and vulnerable and defenseless.

Not at all old enough to become the mother of twins.

Twins!

"God."

He said the word aloud without meaning to, and at the sound of it she jerked. Her eyes opened and she blinked rapidly. "Oh!" She sat upright, folded her hands again, and tried to look as if she hadn't just been sound asleep. "S-sorry. I... It's the heat. And I'm just a little tired and..." She stopped, still looking flustered.

"Here's the tea." He handed it to her then crossed the room and sat down in the armchair opposite her. "Why'd you go out today? Were you doing an interview?"

"Yes." She took a sip of the tea and straightened up against the sofa back again, but she didn't seem as stiff as before. "With Mooney Vaughan."

"Wow." He knew what a coup that was. He was a big name. A very popular entertainer. The two of them had gone to hear him once last summer at Carnegie Hall. After, Rhys remembered, they'd gone up the Empire State

Building again, the music still singing in their minds. It had been a star-filled night and…

He forced himself back to the present. ''Did he play for you?''

Mariah smiled. ''He did. It was wonderful. He's just like his music,'' she said. ''He has this *energy,* this enthusiasm. He's seen some difficult times…you know he lost that son in an accident and his wife, well, you know about the drugs… He's had heartbreak. But he was just so…I don't know…steady. That seems like too simple a word. He wasn't at all Pollyannaish. Of course, you wouldn't expect him to be. But he wasn't bitter or cynical either. He talked about it all—you could hear the pain. But alongside it there was such…hope.''

Her eyes grew soft as she spoke. There was this gentle, understanding smile on her face. It was a smile Rhys knew well. It had been a part of his life for the past three years. It had gentled and soothed him. He studied the bottle in his hands, remembering.

Mariah giggled suddenly. It was such a soft, happy sound that Rhys looked up, surprised to hear her laughter. ''What?''

She looked down and pressed a hand against her abdomen. ''He kissed my belly.''

''What?'' He gaped at her now.

She looked at him, still smiling. ''For luck,'' she said. ''As a blessing. He said it was always a pleasure to be in the company of new life. And he…he played them…us…a song.'' She swallowed and her smile seemed to tremble all at once. She blinked rapidly.

Then she put the glass down on the end table and started to get to her feet. ''I don't think I should stay.''

Rhys was out of his chair before she was off the sofa, blocking her way. ''Yes,'' he said firmly. ''You should.''

She looked at him. Their gazes caught. "Please, Mariah. Stay."

She stayed.

It was foolish. It was a mistake. She knew it would make her want all the things she'd wanted for so long and knew very well she couldn't have.

But, as always, she was powerless against him when he looked at her with those fathomless blue eyes and asked her to do something.

She stayed. She shared the meal with him.

He put on a Mooney Vaughan CD and the music seemed to fit her mood. Buoyant one minute, wistful the next. Highs and lows. Fasts and slows.

"The whole emotional register, that's what I'm after," Mooney had said to her that afternoon, his soft low voice like rough silk.

Mariah's whole emotional register was in play tonight. She couldn't stop it. Couldn't maintain the distance, the indifference she knew she ought to strive for.

She didn't know if she could ever be truly indifferent to Rhys. She knew him too well. Had loved him too long.

She'd tried to fight her feelings for him for the past three years. She'd told herself that she was doing a good job. And spending all those evenings with Kevin had distracted her.

But they hadn't changed the way she felt.

But they hadn't changed the way Rhys felt, either. She knew that. She could see it in him. He was still Rhys. Still easygoing and funny, insightful and quick, intense and passionate. All of those things by turns.

When he let himself go.

When he forgot that things had changed, that *she* had changed—that she was carrying his babies in her womb.

And she could see every time he remembered, whenever

his gaze dropped to her belly, when he started to speak, then stopped and his tone of voice changed, flattened, when almost imperceptibly, but very definitely, he withdrew.

And then, she knew, he was remembering. Not just her and the babies, but the past—and that earlier baby—the ones he loved and couldn't let go.

Mariah wanted to cry then. She didn't. She had more of a sense of self-preservation than that. She didn't say anything—or she said something that drew his attention away, that made him smile and change the subject.

She survived the evening.

She thanked him politely. She tolerated, was actually grateful for him lugging her carryall up to her flat. She thanked him for that, too.

He just nodded. "Take care of yourself, Mariah."

"I will," she said. "Thanks again." And then she added airily, "See you around," as if they were friends again.

Maybe they were.

But when she went to bed that night she cried.

He didn't see her the next morning.

He wasn't really looking. It was just that the light was good if he sat in the chair by the window while he did the crossword from the *Times*. And he couldn't help it if he could see the stairs. He saw Mrs. Alvarez go up and down four times. And he saw the Gillespies, the married couple who had the floor through on the floor above Mariah. And he saw their cleaning lady, and Mrs. Alvarez's cousin, Consuelo.

But he didn't see Mariah.

Probably out with Kevin, he thought. He dragged his mind away from that and focused on the crossword again. His pencil lead snapped.

"The hell with it," he muttered and hauled himself to his feet. He wandered through the apartment and out into his small back garden. His tomatoes were ripe. He'd put some in the salad last night. He picked a few more now.

Then he heard a noise up on Mariah's terrace and saw her hanging out her laundry again. Just her. No Kevin.

"Hey," he called to her.

She looked over the railing.

"I'll bring you some tomatoes!" He didn't stop to see if she wanted any. He just gathered what he had and went back in, putting them in a bag.

When she opened the door he shoved it at her. "They're more yours than mine anyway. If you hadn't watered them…" he shrugged and gave her a wry grin "…well, they owe their life to you."

"So now you're giving them to me to eat them? Hardly seems fair."

"Life is tough when you're a tomato."

They stared at each other. Awareness pulsed.

"You look…better today," he said finally. "Not that you didn't look great yesterday. But…" He shrugged helplessly.

"I looked wrung out yesterday. I *was* wrung out yesterday. Thank you for the tomatoes." She didn't invite him in. In fact she looked as if she was about to close the door when she suddenly said, "Oh!" and Rhys saw the bag jerk in her hands.

"What's wrong?"

Mariah smiled slightly. "He…or she…kicked me."

Rhys's eyes went straight to the bulge behind the bag of tomatoes. Mariah held the bag away and flattened her shirt against her belly. "Watch."

He watched. Stared, fascinated, as indeed her belly seemed to ripple of its own accord.

"Weird, huh?"

Rhys's mouth was dry. He opened his mouth to speak, but could think of nothing to say. Weird? Yes.

And suddenly sharply painful. It brought back the memories all over again.

Memories of the day Sarah had first felt the life of their child. She'd grabbed his hand and pressed it against her abdomen.

"Feel? Can you feel it, Rhys?" Her eyes had been shining and eager, wanting to share this miracle with him.

He'd pressed and waited. But the flutterings had been too light. The baby still too tiny. The movements had been too weak to be felt, much less seen. Finally he'd shaken his head.

Sarah had kissed him in consolation. "Soon," she'd promised. "You'll feel them soon. It won't be long."

But it had been forever.

A week later Sarah was dead.

His throat worked now. He turned away from Mariah whose belly was still rippling. "I have to go."

They were always there—the memories. Ready to blindside every moment. Ready to come out of nowhere and destroy any moments she and Rhys might share.

Mariah wanted to throw his damn tomatoes. She wanted to kick the door. Or kick him!

But she couldn't. She couldn't even rage at him. She knew his pain.

She recalled too well the night he'd told her about Sarah and the baby. She remembered far too clearly the thick, harsh ache in his voice. She'd seen the pain and heard the unshed tears.

How could she be angry at a man who cared that much, a man who'd lost so much? She couldn't.

But still she couldn't help feeling that it wasn't fair.

It wasn't her fault Rhys had lost the woman he loved and the child she bore!

But it was her fault, she reminded herself, that he was becoming a father again.

"It was his fault, too," she muttered as she carried the tomatoes into the kitchen. That was only the truth.

But mostly it was hers.

If she hadn't gone down that night…if she hadn't held out her arms to him…if she hadn't loved him…

One of the babies kicked her.

And she knew that the ifs didn't matter anymore. It was too late for if.

She patted her belly. "You're here and I'm glad you're here," she told her unborn children fiercely. "And if I need reminding you just go right ahead and kick me."

Pity, she thought, that they couldn't kick her where she needed it—in the butt.

CHAPTER SEVEN

HE WENT back to work.

He called his boss the next day. He asked, "You need me anywhere?" and got himself sent to Turkey—just like that. Rhys packed his bag before six and left before midnight. He didn't even tell anyone he was going.

It wasn't until he'd been in Turkey three days that he finally called Dominic to tell him where he was.

"You're where? Turkey? What are you telling me for?" Dominic sounded impatient, harassed and totally uninterested in where his brother might be. Rhys heard him cover the mouthpiece of the phone and bark, "Tell him now. Just no!" at his secretary. Then he came back to Rhys. "What are you telling me for?"

Why was he telling Dominic? He never had before.

"I...er...just thought you ought to know. In case something happens," Rhys said. "To Dad."

"Like I kill him?"

"Whoa. That bad, is it? What's he doing now?"

"Breathing down my neck. He's got a new girl every damn week. Keeps parading 'em through the office. I can't get any work done. I need to throw up a roadblock, find a woman of my own."

"To marry?"

"Maybe," Dominic said, shocking him. "If we like each other. Know any available women?"

"No."

"Of course you do. Footloose fellow like you. You must have a girl in every port."

"Not for you to marry."

"What about your neighbor?"

"Who? Mariah?" Rhys's whole body tensed.

"Yeah, Mariah. She's a fox. She'd sure as hell make the old man back off. I wouldn't mind marrying Mariah."

"No!"

The force of Rhys's reply caused complete silence five thousand two hundred miles away. "Oh," Dominic said shortly, reading way too much into Rhys's exclamation. "Like that, is it?"

"No, it's not like that!" Rhys denied hotly. "It's just…"

But he couldn't say she was pregnant. That would really have Dominic wanting to know who the father was—and making a very well educated guess. It also wouldn't be beyond Dominic to mention the fact to their father, to take a little of the heat off himself for a while.

"It's just that Mariah deserves better. She doesn't deserve a loveless marriage."

"And you aren't interested?"

"I'm a one-woman man."

There was another long pause. Then Dominic said, "Sarah's been gone a long time. She wouldn't expect you to—"

"I'm not interested," Rhys said harshly. "Just drop it, okay?"

"Just saying," Dominic replied, his tone mild. "Don't bite my head off."

"Don't push me, then. And forget Mariah."

Dominic didn't push. He mentioned a couple of other women who might be useful decoys. "Anyone to keep the old man at bay. I don't know where he finds these women."

"A deep freeze?" Rhys guessed. He was wishing he hadn't called. A niggling little part of his brain told him that maybe he *should* suggest to Dominic that he contact Mariah.

Maybe they would hit it off. Maybe she could marry Dominic and keep the kids "in the family," as it were.

Rhys's whole being recoiled at the thought. He didn't want his brother anywhere near Mariah.

He didn't stop to think about the reason for that.

He was gone.

Just like that. Overnight. One day he was there, the next he was not.

At first Mariah just thought Rhys was lying low, doing his best—and succeeding—in avoiding her. Then she realized that the angle of his blinds never changed, that his lights came on like clockwork—and no one was watering his tomatoes.

He was gone.

The hell with him, she thought.

She threw herself into her work.

She finished her article about Mooney Vaughan and told Stella she was interested in whatever else came along. Stella called back two days later with a projected story about Simon Hollingsworth, an architect and designer who had done some of the most innovative work on the east coast.

Mariah went up to Cape Cod for four days to interview Simon. He invited her to Martha's Vineyard to see the project he was working on, then she spent two days with him in Newport looking at some renovations he'd done.

He mentioned other places he'd worked on—on Block Island, along the coast of Maine, down in Virginia. Mariah visited them all. It was exhilarating, demanding. It kept her going long hours.

Hours she didn't have to think about Rhys.

When she got home, she concentrated on the writing. That was more difficult. And not just because of Rhys.

It was harder to sit at the computer. Her belly was bigger.

It got in the way. The babies were more active. They
wanted to kick and play whenever she tried to sit still and
work.

So she went for long walks. Kevin sometimes went with
her. They talked about his girlfriend. They talked about the
stories she was working on. They talked about the babies.
They never talked about Rhys.

Mariah didn't let herself think about Rhys. It was a question of mind over mind, she assured herself. If she kept her
mind occupied with other things, he wouldn't have a
chance to creep in.

The trouble was, she couldn't research and write and go
for long walks all the time. Some of the time she had to
go to bed, to try to sleep. But sleeping wasn't easy. The
babies seemed destined to become nocturnal kickboxers, at
least if their prenatal behavior was anything to go by.

They kicked and punched their way through most of the
hours between midnight and five a.m. But even if they
hadn't she would have had to get up anyway. She always
needed to go to the bathroom.

''You know how they say you're eating for two?'' she
said to Sierra one afternoon when her sister dropped by and
commented on the dark circles under her eyes and the
weary look on Mariah's face. ''Well, I'm peeing for three.
And we all seem to need to get up at different times.''

''You look exhausted,'' Sierra said frankly. ''Like one
of those Halloween spooks.''

''Thank you very much.''

''Well, you usually look so healthy. Now you look
scrawny and pale.''

''Scrawny? How can I look scrawny when I feel like a
beached whale?''

''The scrawny part is you. The beached whale bit are
those freeloaders who are going to be your children. Pity
Rhys can't lug them around for a while.''

Mariah didn't respond to that. She knew the mention of Rhys was a probe to find out how things stood now. Mariah hoped if she didn't answer the question would never be asked.

She should have known better.

"Have you heard from the father of your children?" Sierra asked when she didn't get anywhere with the more subtle approach.

"He's working."

"Bully for him. Has he called you? Does he know you're dragging around looking awful?"

"Well, I certainly haven't told him!"

"So he hasn't called." Sierra could read between the lines. She studied her sister closely. "Maybe you should take some time off."

"No."

"Why not? You need to get some rest."

"I need to keep food on the table. I'm my sole support."

"Rhys—"

"Rhys is not supporting me! I wouldn't let him. Besides, I love my work. And people expect my byline. They look forward to it. Stella said so just the other day."

"When's Rhys coming back?"

Mariah shrugged. "I don't know. I don't care. He's not involved."

"The two of you should have your heads knocked together," Sierra said bluntly. "I don't know who's dumber—him for not wanting to get involved or you for letting him get away with it. The babies—"

"Are fine. Stop worrying. Honestly, you're as bad as Mom."

A comparison that was a surefire way to get Sierra to stop doing anything.

Now she said, "Mom's worried, too? Well, for once she's absolutely right."

*   *   *

While Rhys worked, he didn't have to think.

When he was off, he was usually too tired to do more than have a beer with a buddy, then hit the sack.

It should have been exactly what he needed.

And it would have been—without the dreams.

Every night there were dreams. Dreams of Sarah. Collages of their life together—happy childhood moments, the joy of their engagement, the bliss of their wedding day. There were a hundred moments—a thousand memories—all coming to wash over him the second he shut his eyes and gave in to slumber.

And they made him ache with longing. And he awoke sad and desperate—reaching for something—for some-one—who slipped further and further away.

Those were bad. Worse, though, were his dreams of Mariah. In them he saw her laughing and smiling, joyful and tender. Her eyes watched him, her hands touched him. And in his dreams he responded. His body grew ready for hers. His heart grew hungry for hers. His arms lifted to reach out to her.

And then he would see Sarah again. Drifting just out of reach.

Then, always, he woke up. Alone.

Mariah was tired.

She was more than tired. She was beat. She and Sierra had painted the room that was going to be the nursery this week. She'd bought two cribs and a dresser. She'd made curtains and had hung them, which had been the biggest challenge of all. But her exhaustion had less to do with physical exertion and lack of sleep than it did with worry. It was the worry that was getting to her, that was making her crazy.

The fear that, despite the brave face she was putting on, she was not going to be able to make it alone.

How was she going to get any work done at all once they were born? In six weeks, if she went full term, she would find out. It was a terrifying thought.

At least now they didn't require changing and feeding every couple of hours. They were there, kickboxing their little hearts out, but at least they were silent. When they were born, they would cry, they would need to eat, they would need to be changed. She would have to do a thousand loads of laundry and go grocery shopping and cook meals and clean the apartment on top of doing the work that brought in money.

And how could she travel with the babies? How could she go to Martha's Vineyard or Newport or…wherever?

How on earth was she going to cope?

The very thought of trying to deal with it all was almost enough to do her in.

Of course, Rhys had said he would provide financial support for the children. And she was grateful.

But she couldn't let him support her. She would have to do that.

And she didn't know how she was going to manage.

All she could think of was working her butt off now—so that she could afford to take some time off when the babies were born.

Stella was delighted. "The more the better," she said. "I can save the articles and put them out over several months. Go for it."

Mariah went for it.

She worked. She wrote. She peed. The babies moved. They shifted. They kicked.

"I think I have a field goal specialist on board," she told Kevin when he dropped by to see if she wanted to go out to dinner.

It was one of those unseasonably warm November days, the ones that encouraged you to spend them outside because, with any shift in the wind, chances were that old man winter would come breathing down your neck and you wouldn't get another nice day until spring.

So Mariah had spent it out on the terrace, cleaning up what was left of the plants in her flower boxes, then sitting at the small table, working on her laptop, trying to finish up the rough draft of the story she'd spent the past two days in Philly getting.

She'd interviewed a pianist who lived on the top floor of an old warehouse in which the elevator had been out of commission. She'd hiked up six flights of stairs, lugging her carryall with tape recorder and notepads. Her back had ached all the way home. It persisted still.

She'd come home this morning and tried to write, but the babies had kicked a lot, so she'd worked on the flower boxes to keep moving. Then she'd gone for a walk to try to settle them down.

But nothing had settled them. She wondered sometimes if they kept each other awake as much as they kept her from sleeping.

"Or maybe they've taken up clogging," she told Kevin.

He looked horrified. "Clogging? Cripes," he muttered. "Maybe you don't want to go out to dinner, then."

"No. I would like to go." Getting out would be good. Better than staying home and trying to work while her unborn children auditioned for Riverdance in her abdomen.

Besides, she didn't want to turn Kevin away. Even though she didn't need him to deflect Rhys anymore, he still came by to see her a couple of times a week, and she was just glad to have him around. He was a good friend.

She put away her laptop. She could finish the article after she came home or tomorrow morning. Rubbing her back, she fetched her jacket. "Let's go," she said.

They went to a small quiet Italian place just off Columbus. It was a nice place to just relax and enjoy a meal, nothing frenetic, nothing demanding. Perfect, Mariah thought, and she tried to focus on what Kevin was saying.

But her back really hurt and she couldn't get comfortable. She felt a tightening across her abdomen.

"What?" Kevin said.

"Huh? Oh, nothing. They're just squeezing."

He looked baffled. "Squeezing?"

"That's what it feels like." She studied the menu. The waiter came and they gave their order. And Mariah felt the sensation again. She shifted in her chair. They were not the world's most comfortable chairs.

"You okay?" Kevin asked.

She nodded, shifting again. The kickboxers weren't happy. Maybe they needed to pee. She got up. "I'll be right back." She went to the bathroom downstairs. She felt the tightening again as she went.

She stayed down there a long time. Ten minutes. The tightening was occurring every three. With regularity.

She was shaking when she came back to the table.

Kevin saw it at once. "What's wrong?"

"I think I'm having the babies."

"No," Mariah said.

She glared up at her sister and said it again. She'd been saying it since Sierra had met her and Kevin at the hospital last night. "No, Sierra! I don't know where Rhys is. I don't know how to get in touch with him. I don't *want* to get in touch with him!"

"You need to," Sierra said. She stood over Mariah's bed now and, hands on hips, glared right back down at her sister who plucked irritably at the sheet and tried to think calm, cheerful, relaxing thoughts like the doctor had told her to do.

It wasn't working—because Sierra kept right on pestering.

"Telling him won't do any good," Mariah said firmly. "Besides," she added, looking away out the window, "he won't want to know. Because something *happening* to me or to the babies is exactly what he doesn't want to have to face." Mariah sighed. "It happened before," she explained.

She'd never told Sierra about Rhys's wife and child. He'd made it clear that he didn't want his past discussed, and there had never been any reason to before. Now Mariah knew her sister wouldn't leave well enough alone until she had a compelling reason.

So briefly, going into as little detail as possible, she told her sister about Rhys's wife, about the baby they were going to have. And about how he'd lost them both—and couldn't forgive himself or forget or move on.

"So you see why he can't get involved," she finished. She gave Sierra a faint smile.

"The hell I do! All I see is what a selfish ass he is!" Sierra flounced around the room, practically bouncing off the walls. "His wife died and so that gives him an excuse to be a jerk to the woman he got pregnant?"

"You don't understand," Mariah said wearily.

"No, I damned well don't!" Sierra fumed. She muttered. Mariah thought smoke might easily come out her ears. "You're having twins! You almost *had* twins last night. You need to be taken care of—not taking care of someone else!"

"I'm not taking care of him! I'm just saying I don't need him," she said in an effort to placate Sierra. "I don't need anyone." She tried to sound put-together, capable, calm.

Sierra wasn't buying. "Bull," she said. "You need bed rest and calm and someone to do everything for you."

"Not Rhys."

Sierra glowered. She did another lap around Mariah's

bedroom. Mariah shut her eyes so she wouldn't have to watch.

"Look," Mariah said finally, with as much patience as she could muster, "you're not exactly promoting a stress-free existence here. You look like you're going to blow up. Just go away and let me sleep."

Sierra stopped pacing and looked contrite. "I'm sorry. But—" She caught herself. "I'll shut up. You get some rest. I'll just be out in the other room."

"You don't have to stick around."

"Yes, I do. And unless you want to fight about it, go to sleep."

And Mariah knew there was no arguing with the pugnacious Kelly chin when it lifted like that.

"I'll be fine," she whispered as Sierra gave her a quick kiss on the forehead. She smiled until her sister left the room. Then she closed her eyes and prayed that it was true.

She'd been praying ever since the contractions had started and Kevin had taken her to the hospital straight from the restaurant the night before.

The hospital had called her doctor and he'd come right in. He'd examined her, murmuring and muttering, while Mariah had stared at him in white-faced, dry-mouthed panic.

"Am I...? Are they...?" But she couldn't even voice her deepest fears.

Finally he'd looked at her over the top of his glasses. "You, my dear, need to take it easy."

"I will," she'd promised fervently. "But...are they all right?"

"So far. We need to stop those contractions." And then he'd insisted she stay in the hospital overnight. "Just to make sure nothing starts going wrong."

Thank God, nothing had.

She'd lain awake all night, barely daring to move. Trying to accomplish the almost impossible, which was to relax.

Kevin had called Sierra and the two of them had sat there all night, not relaxed, right along with her.

Finally, though, the rhythmic tightening across her abdomen had slowed and eased. By morning it had become faint and irregular.

When the doctor came in, he'd been pleased. "So far so good," he had said. Then he'd shaken his finger at her. "But from here on out you have to be careful."

"I'll be careful," Mariah had promised.

"Rest. In bed. All week. After that, if everything is okay, you can be up and around. No overdoing," he said sternly. "No taking on the world."

"I won't."

"You can't," he said firmly. "These babies are getting big and restless and they're creating stress of their own. And, from what your sister has said, you're working very hard." Sierra had been her usual vocal self about how hard Mariah was working.

"I'll stop."

"Yes," the doctor and Sierra had said together, "you will."

"You're caught in the middle," the doctor went on. "I know that. But you have to take care of yourself. Rest. Sleep. Eat. Get fat and lazy. You do that, you'll be fine."

"All of us?" Mariah asked, her heart in her throat.

"Another month and these babies will have a much better chance."

"Wolfe? Phone." The voice came out to Rhys in the darkness.

It was sometime in the middle of the night where he was. Singapore? Saudi Arabia? Taiwan? It would come to him when he got more of his brain cells together.

Turkey. Yeah, Turkey.

Phone? Who the hell would be calling him?

Mariah.

He was out of bed and stumbling toward the doorway. "Thanks, Blake," he said to the guy who'd called him and who pointed him in the direction of the one lone telephone in the place.

"Mariah?" he barked when he grabbed it up.

"Right in one," his brother Dominic drawled.

Rhys clutched the phone in a death grip. "What happened? Is she…?"

"She's okay. Now."

Rhys let out a harsh breath and sagged against the wall. "Then what the hell are you—? How do you know about Mariah?" he demanded.

"I got a little visit."

"From Mariah?" Rhys couldn't imagine.

"No. Her sister. You didn't tell me she was pregnant," Dominic growled. "More important, you didn't tell me you had a vested interest, shall we say, in the, er, input…as well as in the outcome."

"Tell me!"

"She was having contractions. It's not—"

"*What?* Already? What happened? Is she all right?"

"She's getting along fine at the moment," Dominic said, his voice more soothing now. "She was in the hospital overnight as a precaution. She's home now. In bed. It was a…warning, I guess you'd say. She has to take it easy."

"Damn right she does," Rhys muttered. Wasn't that what he'd been saying all along?

"Rest. Sleep. Put her feet up."

"Of course."

"The purple-haired witch doesn't think she'll do it."

"You *met* Sierra? You talked to her in your office?"

"Sierra," Dominic corrected, "talked to me. Shouted at

me. Stomped past my secretary, burst into my office, grabbed me by the tie and told me she'd wrap it around a certain part of my anatomy and twist if I didn't get hold of you right now and tell you to get your butt home and take care of her sister.''

''Whoa,'' Rhys said.

''Wow,'' Rhys said.

''Yeah,'' Rhys said with dawning admiration, ''I can see Sierra doing something like that.''

It didn't take much imagination at all to envision Mariah's nutty sister knocking Dominic's very proper secretary for a loop, then tackling the CEO of Wolfe Enterprises on his own turf. Another time he could have entertained himself for hours with the scenario.

Now he said, ''I'm on my way.''

''Glad to hear it, Dad,'' Dominic drawled.

Dad.

Rhys didn't think about that.

He didn't think about anything but getting back to Mariah. They owed him time. He'd come in early.

It was a family emergency, he told his boss. And he got the next plane to London. He had a short layover there, then he caught a non-stop to New York. He was home practically before he left—at least according to the clock.

In fact, he had no idea what time it was—anywhere.

He was operating entirely on automatic by the time he got out of the cab in front of his brownstone the next evening. He tossed his bag in his front door and pounded up the stairs.

His hammering on Mariah's door got no response.

He felt a renewed sense of panic. What if she was in the hospital? What if she'd had the babies? They wouldn't survive, would they, being so early? Would *she* survive?

He pounded again. 'Damn it!'' he said through his teeth. ''Open the damn door!''

And then, at last, he heard the lock turn and the chain rattle. The door opened a crack. He expected to see Sierra.

Mariah stared back at him, astonished. ''What are you—?''

He didn't wait for the question. Didn't answer it at all.

He pushed the door open and strode past her into the room. She was wearing a pair of baggy shorts and a sweat-shirt—and even though it had been less than a month since he'd seen her she'd changed again.

Or rather her belly had. It was huge.

''What are you doing out of bed?'' he demanded.

Still she gaped at him, then she almost visibly pulled herself together. ''I was answering the door,'' she said starchily. ''Some idiot was pounding on it.''

''I thought Sierra would be here.''

''Sierra has a life.''

''She won't when I get done with her. What the hell does she mean, leaving you alone?''

''I beg your pardon?''

''Go get in bed,'' Rhys said, moving in on her, herding her toward the bedroom even as he spoke. ''You're sup-posed to be lying down.''

''Says who?''

''Sierra. The doctor. My brother.''

''Your brother? *Dominic?*'' Mariah's jaw dropped. ''What's Dominic got to do with this?''

''He called me.''

''Whatever for?''

''To preserve his virility, I believe. Sierra threatened it unless he tracked me down.''

''I'll kill her.''

''No, you won't. Too much stress. Damn it, Mariah. Go

lie down!'' And when she didn't immediately he took her
by the arm and steered her toward the bedroom.

She resisted for just a second, then sighed. ''You really
are a bully,'' she muttered as she allowed herself to be
shoved down the hallway. ''I don't know what you're doing here. He shouldn't have called you.''

''Yes, he should have.'' He backed her toward the bed
and nodded, satisfied, when she sat down abruptly. ''Feet
up.''

''I don't—''

''Feet up!'' He bent and took hold of her calves, lifting
her feet onto the bed. Then he sank down beside her and
sprawled on the bed.

''Rhys!''

''Mmm?'' He flung one arm over her to make her stay
put, then shut his eyes.

''What do you think you're doing?''

''Taking care of you,'' he murmured.

She tried shoving his arm off, but he went totally limp,
half from exhaustion and half from perverseness.

''I don't need 'taking care of,''' she argued.

''Not what I heard,'' he mumbled. He rolled onto his
side and hauled her close. God, she felt good. A hell of a
lot better than his pillow which he'd woken up hugging
recently. He tucked his arm more tightly around her burgeoning middle.

It kicked him.

He jerked his head up. ''What the hell—?''

''You were squishing them, Mariah said tartly.

''Them? Huh? Oh!'' He loosened his grip, flattened his
palm against her belly. It shifted and rolled beneath his
hand. Them. The children.

His children.

He didn't want to think about that.

Not now.

He couldn't think about anything now. He was here. That was enough.

"Are they like that all the time?" he mumbled.

"Not all the time. Sometimes they sleep."

"Good." He settled in again, fitting his body to curve against hers, anchoring her loosely with his arm. "Thank God for that."

"Rhys!"

But he shut his eyes and went to sleep.

CHAPTER EIGHT

HE WENT to sleep!

He burst into her apartment, pinned her to her bed—*and fell asleep*!

Mariah twisted beneath his arm and edged back to lie watching Rhys now.

He looked exhausted. Drained. There were dark shadows under his eyes and a drawn look on his face, even in sleep. Where had he come from? How long had he been traveling?

And what on earth compelled a man who didn't want to be bothered to come from...from...wherever just to boss her around?

Surely Sierra wouldn't have really carried through with her threat to emasculate his brother!

She might have tried, Mariah thought with a wry smile. But Mariah had met Dominic Wolfe. He was not a man to be easily intimidated—even by a purple-haired virago.

Perhaps Dominic had strong-armed Rhys into it. Yes. Very likely that was it.

Dominic Wolfe had an enormous sense of family responsibility. He worked in the family business, dealt with his bossy, pushy father, took his lumps, and kept coming back—all for the good of the family.

She knew that, long ago, he'd even been going to marry to please his father, not himself.

She didn't know much more about it than that because Rhys didn't tell many tales. But he had said that Dominic took his duty to his family very seriously.

Obviously he thought Rhys should do likewise.

And so, clearly, did Sierra.

Mariah didn't think her sister had ever met Rhys's brother. She hadn't thought Sierra even knew who he was.

Apparently she'd found out. Sierra, when she made up her mind, could move heaven and earth to accomplish something. Once she'd made up her mind to find Rhys, she would have done so—any way she could.

Mariah sighed. She should have known her sister wouldn't have given up when she'd shut up about needing to find Rhys. She'd had too many other things on her mind, too many important things—like the health and well-being of her children—to pay attention to her sister.

She should have tied Sierra to a chair.

"Yeah, you and whose army?" she murmured.

"Mmm? Huh?" Rhys muttered now in his sleep. He tucked his hand around her middle possessively. As if it belonged there. As if she belonged to him.

Mariah felt her throat tighten. She swallowed hard against the lump that formed there. "Damn," she muttered softly, her lips inches from Rhys's. "Oh, damn. Why did you have to come back?"

How could she fight him when she had no strength left?

"G'sleep," Rhys murmured.

She shouldn't.

But she couldn't help it. Mariah sighed and settled back against him, letting the curve of his body cradle hers. His hand eased away from her abdomen and pressed lightly against her breasts.

She reached for it, took it in hers and drew it to her lips. Then once more she tucked it against her belly.

And then she, too, slept.

The first hint of sunlight peeking in the window woke him.

It happened like that sometimes, when his internal clock became so befuddled it didn't know where he was or what time it was. It relied on the sun then and woke him no matter how long he had—or hadn't—been asleep.

It happened that way now. And Rhys had no idea where he was or why—until he rolled over and bumped against the warm body of a woman.

His eyes flickered open. And then he remembered—and wished he hadn't.

Because the woman was Mariah. And he was in her bed.

It came back to him then.

Dominic's phone call. His own call to his boss, his dash to the airport, cooling his heels in London, worrying, wondering…and finally his arrival last night.

He'd never been so glad to see anybody up and around and looking reasonably healthy and still very, very pregnant in his life.

He hadn't wanted to worry about her. But he had.

He would, he was sure now—until these babies were safely born. Until Mariah was through this pregnancy. Until, however much it changed, she had her life back.

It was up to him to see that that happened.

Then he could back off. Then he could walk away.

But, right now, this wasn't about him.

It was about her.

Her. Mariah. He lifted up on one elbow so he could see her better in the dim morning light. There were dark circles under her eyes. Her normally rosy cheeks looked pale—the way they'd looked when she'd taken a whiff of that fish.

It wasn't fish causing this. It was stress—too much worry, too much work, too much of everything, from what little Dominic had told him.

Well, Rhys could take care of that. He could take care of her.

He would do his bit—exactly as he'd promised he would. He'd see her through this.

Then he would go.

* * *

"I don't know why you want to come to the doctor with me," Mariah grumbled. She was trying to put on her shoes, a major challenge when she couldn't even see her feet—but she looked up long enough to flick a glance in his direction, one designed to communicate her wish that he would just go away.

Of course, he didn't move. He'd been sitting in that chair ever since she'd opened her eyes, and it seemed as if he was watching her every move. She finally retreated into the bathroom to dress. But she still felt awkward and ill-at-ease.

And, oh, damn, why didn't he just leave?

"I want to find out what he thinks," Rhys said reasonably. As if it were reasonable to suddenly drop into her pregnancy after seven and a half months and act as if he cared!

Mariah didn't want him to care!

Well, no, that wasn't quite true. She did want him to care. But for the right reasons—for reasons of love and a genuine desire to be with her—and their children—for the rest of their lives.

That wasn't why he was here.

He'd already explained why he was here. "Because you need me," he'd said.

And all the arguing in the world hadn't changed his mind on that.

Well, maybe the doctor would. She dared to hope.

But she found out an hour and a half later that the doctor was no use at all. In fact, he and Rhys seemed determined to complicate her life even more.

The doctor was delighted to meet him.

About time, his expression said when Rhys introduced himself as the father of her children and said he was concerned about what was happening.

In the beginning of her pregnancy, the doctor had asked

questions about Rhys's medical history, but once he'd asked if the babies' father was going to be "involved," and she'd said no, he'd been discreet and polite, unintrusive and nonjudgmental.

Apparently that didn't preclude his being thrilled at the notion that Rhys was behaving in the time-honored role of the arrogant-male-taking-charge at last.

He shooed Rhys out while he checked Mariah over, nodding and muttering to himself. Then he called Rhys in again and spelled everything out.

"She needs total rest," the doctor said to him, just as if Mariah wasn't there. "No stairs. No lifting over twenty pounds. No climbing on ladders or lugging groceries. She needs to sit back, put her feet up and be waited on twenty-four hours a day."

"I do not!" Mariah objected.

But the doctor, warming to his task, went right on. "She needs lots of TLC because if she doesn't get it these babies are going to come early and that won't be good."

"She'll get it," Rhys vowed.

"I am getting it," Mariah said.

"My brother has a place out on Long Island, about an hour from here," Rhys told the doctor. "I'll take her out there."

"You will not," Mariah said.

"All one level. Right on the beach. About ten minutes from the local hospital. Not that I expect it will be necessary."

"Sounds perfect," said her doctor.

"She'll get a lot of rest. And I won't let her do anything stupid."

Mariah glared at Rhys. "The stupidest thing I ever did was—"

"Thanks very much," Rhys said to the doctor, cutting Mariah right off. "Pleasure to meet you."

"You, too." They shook hands like old friends. "I want to see her again in two weeks."

"I don't need—" Mariah began.

But the doctor was already gone.

"I'm not going out to any house of your brother's," Mariah told Rhys sharply as they went out through the waiting room.

He waited until they were out on the street before answering. "Yes," he said. "You are."

She wasn't. But she wasn't going to argue with him about it. They rode back to the apartment in silence. Mariah kept her arms folded across the top of her belly. They bounced a little because one of the babies was giving her plenty of kicks.

She hoped Rhys didn't notice. She slanted a glance his way, but it was hard to tell if he was noticing or not. He had sunglasses on and his eyes were hidden. She wished she knew what he was thinking, then thought it was better that she didn't. She doubted he'd be thinking anything she wanted to know.

He didn't speak until they got out of the taxi. She headed right up the steps while he paid the driver. If he wanted to come along, fine, he could pay the fare. She was just opening the door when he caught up with her and took her by the arm.

"Didn't you listen?" he demanded.

"You mean while you two talked right over the top of me?"

"While the doctor talked about what you need to do— and not do. Like climb stairs."

"I live upstairs!"

"Not anymore."

"What?" She stared at him, flabbergasted.

"No stairs. That's what he said. That's one reason we're going out to Dominic's."

"We're not going—"

"I thought you wanted these babies." He took off his sunglasses now and looked her square in the face.

Mariah, frowning, took a step back and folded her arms protectively over her belly. "Of course I want them!"

"Then stop being so damn pigheaded. You can't do what you've been doing, Mariah."

"That doesn't mean I have to go to your brother's."

"Well, I suppose we could check into a hotel."

"We could not!" Staying in a hotel was a ridiculous idea. It was prohibitively expensive for one thing, and totally absurd when there were other alternatives. "Chloe—"

"Chloe and Gib have a baby of their own. They don't need to be taking you on."

"Finn and Izzy—"

"Have to climb stairs, too."

"Sierra—"

Rhys just stared at her stonily. They both knew Sierra's fifth-floor walk-up was out of the question.

"I'm not your responsibility," she told him.

He met her gaze, then his lowered to focus on her belly. "They are," he said. "I got you into this, Mariah," he said firmly. "I'm going to see you through it."

Through it. As if they were in some sort of endurance contest. A battle. Something that they would get to the other side of.

Well, she supposed that was the way he saw it.

He tipped her chin up with one finger so that they looked at each other again. "Do it for the children, Mariah."

The children. His children. Someday all she would have left of him.

She drew a breath, then sighed. "All right."

He called Dominic and told him he needed the house. It was the house they'd all grown up in and which Dominic had bought from their father two years ago when the old man ostensibly retired and took himself off to Florida. Their father seemed to be in the city now more than when he'd been officially head of Wolfe Enterprises. But when he was here he preferred to stay in a pied-à-terre in Sutton Place.

"Sure." His brother agreed at once. "Is she...all right?"

"She's fine," Rhys said tersely. "She just needs rest. She's having twins."

"The old man will be—"

"Left out of this. You will not say a word."

"But—"

"No."

"So you're just going to turn your back on 'em?"

"Does it look like I'm turning my back on them?"

"If you won't tell the old man—"

"I'll tell the old man sometime. When I'm good and ready." *When I know he won't be pushing a wedding down my throat.* Because that was exactly what he'd try to do if he found out. And Rhys didn't want a wedding. He didn't want ties.

"Have it your way," Dominic said, but there was a note of disapproval in his voice.

Rhys ignored it. He had other things to think about.

He made Mariah go down to his place and rest. "I'll pack for you."

She started to protest, then shrugged. He was glad. It meant she understood and would go along with what he was trying to do. "Go watch TV or take a nap," he told her. "We can leave after rush hour."

"I can make dinner," she said.

"Order something," he replied. "Sit down, put your feet up. Doctor's orders. Got that?"

He made sure she was sitting, with the TV on and a book

in her hands, before he went upstairs and let himself into her place.

It seemed odd to be there without her. Echoey. Lonely. He went back to her bedroom and began going through her drawers and her closet, picking out clothes for her to wear. He picked the baggiest sweatshirts and trousers with stretchy paneled fronts. He got her bathrobe and her toiletries. He poked through her closet looking for a warm winter jacket and coat. It was November already and the wind would be sharp by the sea.

He found a long wool coat and a hip-length bulky quilted jacket hanging next to a dress he remembered well. It was flame-red, a low-cut silk dress she'd worn to the Christmas party at Finn and Izzy's last year.

He ran his hand over it, remembering that he'd touched it then when they'd danced together. He'd found himself looking down her neckline that night, aware of her breasts, aware of Mariah as a very attractive woman. He lifted it out of the closet now. It was so narrow, so sleek-looking. The Mariah he'd seen at the doctor's today couldn't come close to fitting in it.

He wondered if she ever would. She'd lost her figure to those babies, to the seed he'd put in her. He rubbed his fingers over the silk again and shook his head.

He wondered that she didn't hate him for it.

She didn't like him much, that was clear. She'd been prickly and grumpy since he'd got home. Of course, given the shape she was in, he couldn't see any reason to expect anything different.

He'd just have to make it up to her. Take care of her, like the doc said. See that she got the rest she needed, see that the babies didn't come until they were supposed to.

And after?

He didn't think about that.

* * *

Mariah wasn't used to being pampered.

She wasn't used to having someone wait on her, do for her, fetch for her, bring her hot milk at night and, in the morning, breakfast in bed.

But that was what happened.

Rhys's brother's house was on the south shore of Long Island. It sat on a grassy knoll overlooking the beach and the Atlantic Ocean. It was a low clapboard house with French doors that opened onto a flagstone deck just steps from the sand. It was an old, comfortable family home, not at all what she would have expected of a hard-driving businessman like Rhys's brother Dominic.

She said so and learned that it was the home where Rhys had grown up. That made her look around avidly, at the same time that she told herself she shouldn't. He didn't want to get involved with her. He was only taking care of her because he felt responsible, and it wouldn't do her any good to find more reasons to care about him.

But it was hard not to find them. Especially since he seemed determined every moment to be at her beck and call. He put her in the biggest bedroom. It now belonged to Dominic, but it had once been his parents'. Their wedding picture was still on the wall.

Mariah couldn't help looking at it, couldn't help wishing...

She tried not to. She tried not to look around, tried not to ask for anything.

But Rhys seemed to read her mind. He settled her in the bedroom, grabbed his brother's clothes out of the top two dresser drawers and put her few things in there instead. He brought in a box of books that he'd gathered from her living room and bedroom and he set them in a row on a shelf by the bed.

"I wasn't sure which you were reading and which you'd already read, so I brought 'em all," he said.

She smiled her thanks.

He handed her the remote and showed her how to use it to turn on the television and the stereo in the bedroom. "So you don't even have to get up."

He pointed out the intercom speaker by the bed. "If you need something, you just push the button and talk. I can hear you wherever I am in the house, and I'll get it."

She stared at him, astonished.

"You don't have to move," he told her.

"I'll go crazy," she said.

He shoved his hands into the pockets of his jeans and seemed to seriously consider this possibility. "You can go out on the deck on the afternoons that it's sunny," he decided.

"Thanks," Mariah muttered.

"Can I get you something to eat?" They'd eaten Chinese before they'd left the city, but now it was past ten and that had been a while ago.

Mariah looked at him narrowly, wondering how far he would go. "Pizza?" she said. "With anchovies and Canadian bacon and sauerkraut?"

Rhys swallowed, then nodded. "You got it."

She didn't know where he got it, but half an hour later she heard the doorbell ring, and a few minutes after that he came in bearing a pizza, two plates and two glasses of milk.

She blinked her astonishment when the pizza turned out to have exactly what she'd ordered. She blinked again when Rhys ate three pieces. He licked his fingers after, then downed a glass of the milk.

Mariah ate two pieces and used her napkin.

"Drink your milk," Rhys said.

"I like warm milk before I go to bed," she said out of sheer perversity.

Damned if he didn't take the glass out to the kitchen and come back a few minutes later with warm milk in a mug.

She didn't even like warm milk, but she wasn't admitting it now. She stretched out on the bed and wriggled her toes. She sipped the milk and felt an odd mixture of lethargy and well-being steal over her. She channel-surfed with the remote, skipping over the sporting events just to annoy him.

He just sat there, watching her.

Finally she met his gaze. He was grinning, just a little, as if he knew exactly what she was doing—and why. It made her feel small and ornery—and very much like smiling, too.

So she did.

Because she couldn't help it. Because he was here and so was she—and just now, just for this moment, things were good.

Then she flipped the remote again and found a channel showing a movie in Hungarian. At least she thought it was Hungarian. "Ah," she said. "Perfect."

She didn't understand a word.

He got up and picked up the plates and the pizza and the glass. He left her with her mug of warm milk and her Hungarian movie.

On his way out he smiled at her. "Goodnight."

It was almost like having his life back—the one with Mariah—b.p.

Before pregnancy.

Over the next few days they did things together. Not energetic things. Leisurely things. They figured out the *Times* crossword, they read to each other from books, they looked through old picture albums. He didn't know why she was so fascinated with old photos of him and his brothers growing up, but he didn't mind showing them to her. Didn't mind talking about them, either, if it kept her quiet and entertained. They looked at all the albums but one. The one of his wedding. He didn't take that one down.

Instead he showed her pictures of him playing football and baseball, of him and his brothers building sand castles and bodysurfing in the Bahamas. He told her about the house his parents had bought down there.

It was an old ship's captain's house, he told her. Her journalist's mind was eager for stories. She listened and he told her as many as he could think of.

He'd never talked so much in his life. But she made it easy. She made it almost fun.

And every day she didn't go into labor was one day better for the babies, according to the doc.

He'd put her in the master bedroom because it had a bathroom of its own, a view across the beach to the ocean, and an intercom so she could always get hold of him.

He'd intended to sleep in his own room which was at the far end of the house. But instead he took the room right across the hall from hers. It was now Dominic's study, but it had a sofa that wasn't too hard to sleep on, and he didn't get much sleep anyway.

He was too busy checking on her.

He got up four or five times a night to cross the hall and peek into her room, to see that she was sleeping or, if she was not, to find out if there was anything he could do for her.

"Want a cup of warm milk?" he asked her.

But after that first night she never did.

"It might help you sleep," he told her, but every night she shook her head.

"What would help me sleep is if they would," she grumbled the third night when he heard her pacing around and got up to see what was wrong. She was standing there in the dark, rubbing her abdomen.

He could see her tousle-haired, round-bellied silhouette

in the moonlight, and he remembered how curvy she'd been in that red dress a year ago. But there was something equally appealing about her now. Then she'd looked sexy, now she looked womanly. Then he'd wanted to kiss her and had been surprised at the direction of his thoughts.

They weren't far different now. He stayed right where he was by the door. "They kicking you?"

"They always kick me. But sometimes I can soothe them."

"How?"

She shrugged. "Rubbing my belly sometimes helps." She gave a little laugh. "It's crazy, but I think they like it. Like getting a back rub second hand." She arched her back as she spoke and made a little whimpering sound.

It made Rhys's blood run hot and thick in his veins. He had no business lusting after a pregnant woman, a woman who couldn't possibly be interested in anything of the sort. But it didn't seem to stop him. "You…um…want a back rub?"

She stopped rubbing her belly. "What?"

"You sort of…um…sounded like you thought a back rub might be a good idea. I'll give you one."

Say no, he pleaded silently. *Tell me no.*

"Well, that would be nice," Mariah said.

Be careful what you wish for, Mariah's mother had often said, for you will surely get it.

But a back rub had seemed highly unlikely when she'd tossed and turned and wished for it just half an hour before.

And if anyone had told her Rhys would be offering to give her one, well, she might have laughed out loud.

Oh, he'd been wonderful these past three days. He'd been solicitous and attentive and very much the Rhys she knew and had grown to love. But that Rhys—except that one night—had always kept his hands off.

This one was saying in an almost ragged voice, ''If you want a back rub, lie down and roll over.''

Obediently Mariah did just that. She stretched out on the big bed and rolled onto her side. She tugged the pillow against her belly for support. She rubbed it a little, hoping that the rambunctious twin would be soothed and would relax.

The way she was relaxing?

Uh-huh. She was about as relaxed as a high-tension wire. Her body seemed almost to hum with awareness. All her senses were awake and waiting.

She heard his bare feet on the floor. She felt the mattress shift as he sat beside her.

''Do you have enough room?''

''Yes.''

Outside the surf broke on the beach. But inside her body the blood pounded through her veins, her heart hammered in her chest. And the baby kicked her hard.

''Oof,'' she said. Then, ''Shh,'' she murmured, rubbing her belly again, trying to calm both of them.

''More kicking?''

''Yes.'' She shifted, then reached back and took his hand, pressing it against her belly. Obligingly the baby kicked him.

Rhys went totally still.

Mariah wondered if she'd made a mistake. Maybe he would withdraw now, go back to his own room, leave her alone with them.

But he left his hand there until the baby moved again, and then he kneaded softly. Mariah stiffened in surprise.

Rhys pulled his hand away. ''Sorry.''

She wanted his hand back as soon as it was gone. Would he leave now?

But he didn't. He took her by the shoulders and pressed

his thumbs against her spine. Then he began to massage, to knead his way down vertebra by vertebra.

Mariah whimpered softly.

Rhys stopped. ''What's wrong?''

''N-nothing. Mmm.''

''What's 'mmm' mean?''

''Fine,'' she breathed. ''It means it's fine.''

It was more than fine. It was wonderful. Delicious. Mariah's back arched under the insistent rhythmic pressure of his fingers. She settled her head against the pillow and let herself float. The tension she'd felt began to ease, to slip slowly out of her body. Her lips parted and she breathed deeply, then exhaled slowly on a satisfied sigh. ''Ye-e-es.''

Apparently Rhys needed no translation for that. He kept kneading. It was heavenly. His fingers worked all the way down her spine, then at her waist began to knead at the sides, right where she ached the most.

''Ah-h-h.'' She gave a little shiver of pleasure.

His fingers faltered. ''Um, you all right?''

''Yes. It's wonderful. There. Just there. Do that.''

He did. She felt him shift his weight, move closer. Was that his knee pressing against her butt? Whatever it was it felt hard and warm. Good. His fingers worked, easing the tension, softening the knots, relieving the stress.

Mariah's eyes drifted shut.

She breathed deeply, easily. Her shoulders flexed. Her spine stretched and curved. She could lie here like this forever.

It was so quiet now that she couldn't hear the pounding of her heart any longer. But she could hear Rhys's breathing. It sounded harsh and a little bit quick, as if he'd been running. She wished she could see him. But it was dark. She didn't turn. She let herself float.

Even the babies had quieted now.

She snuggled deeper and gave herself over to the magic of his fingers. They moved slowly, languorously up and down her back and then they reached her shoulders and stilled.

She didn't move.

Then they lifted and she felt a hand stroke her hair. For just an instant it brushed her cheek.

Then something else touched her cheek.

Then he was up and gone. Out the door, just like that.

Mariah reached up a hand to touch her cheek.

It was damp.

CHAPTER NINE

TALK about torture.

What the hell had he been thinking?

Well, he hadn't. Obviously. If he'd thought he would get aroused by merely touching her, he would never have said anything about any damn back rub!

But, Rhys thought, letting himself out the French doors and heading toward the water, who the hell would figure he'd get aroused by simply rubbing his hands over the back of an extraordinarily pregnant, almost comatose woman?

It didn't make any sense!

It didn't make for a good night's sleep, either. Which was why he was stalking across the sand. He'd left Mariah sleeping like the proverbial baby. He supposed he should be glad. That had been the aim of the exercise, after all. And as far as that went he'd been a great success.

He'd also become frustrated beyond belief. He hadn't had a woman in eight months—not since the night he'd slept with Mariah. It hadn't mattered to him somehow. He hadn't wanted it.

Now he wanted it. Wanted *her!* His body ached with desire.

And it was a desire he had no chance of assuaging. There was going to be no consummation. He plunged into the surf and dove straight under an incoming wave in the desperate hope that the icy water would provide a cure.

He came shooting back up, shivering, aching and shocked; something else shocked him more—the sound of his name over the pounding of the waves.

"Rhys!"

He spun around. "What the—? *Mariah?*"

He didn't believe it—but there she came, her body silhouetted against the lights of the house as she tottered, off-balance, toward him across the sand.

He raced back out of the ocean, shaking water as he ran. "What the hell are you doing? You're not supposed to be out here!" He came to a stop inches in front of her and glowered.

She glowered right back. "You're not supposed to swim alone."

He raked a shaking, savage hand through his hair. "For God's sake! I wasn't *swimming!*"

She gave his dripping body a leisurely once-over. "Really?" she said. "Must be my imagination."

They stood there in a face off, so close that he could feel her warm breath on his freezing body, so close that another step and her belly would bump right into him.

She didn't step back, didn't give an inch. And with her dark hair blowing in the moonlight he thought she was the most beautiful damn woman he'd ever seen. A shudder of longing ran through him.

"Cold?" She held out a towel.

Rhys stared at it. Then he dragged his hand down his face and took the towel. He rubbed it briskly over his body. Then he noticed she held something else.

"What's that?"

She looked down, then held it out. It was a life preserver, one of two that hung by the fence.

"You were going to rescue me?" He gaped at her.

She drew herself up haughtily and looked down her nose at him. "If necessary." Her voice was cool and composed. Her hand was shaking.

"God," he muttered. He slung the towel around his neck and took her arm. "Come on. You're supposed to be taking it easy. You're supposed to be asleep."

He was shaking, too, thinking what could have happened to her. "You're crazy, you know that?" he grumbled.

"You should talk." But she leaned against him as they walked and he slipped his arm around her. Her body was warm against his freezing flesh, heating him, starting the fires all over again. But he didn't let himself think about that. He kept a firm hold on her until they were back on the deck, until she'd stopped trembling.

Only then did he drop his arm and step away. "Don't ever do that again," he told her sternly.

"You either," she said.

They stared at each other.

"If you'd…" She didn't finish.

She didn't have to. He read her fear. It wouldn't have happened, he wanted to tell her. Nothing would have happened. But she didn't know that, and she needed him.

"Go to bed, Mariah."

She went.

She'd very nearly made a fool of herself.

No, that was putting too kind a spin on it. She *had* made a fool of herself. She'd actually gone after him with a life preserver—as if she could have saved his life if he'd been drowning!

She didn't know why it had seemed so real a possibility to her. But when he'd left her room she'd listened for the sound of him going across the hall to his own, and instead she'd heard him go out to the living room. And the next thing she'd heard was the sound of the French doors opening and closing.

Curious, she'd got up to look—and had seen him striding across the sand toward the ocean. She'd panicked.

A thousand terrifying thoughts had crowded into her head. What if—? she'd thought. *What if—?*

And so she'd grabbed a towel and that stupid life preserver and she'd gone after him!

Like a fool.

God. A shudder ran through her. She laid a hand on her cheek and could still feel the heat of her embarrassment.

She wouldn't do that again. She needed to get herself together, to stop looking ahead and anticipating disaster.

She heard Rhys come down the hall and she prayed he would go right into his room. Instead he stopped at her door.

"You awake?"

She considered not answering, pretending to be asleep. But then she rolled over. "Yes."

"I brought you a mug of hot milk." He hesitated for a second, then came in and set it on the table in the dark.

"Thank you."

He just stood there. She could feel his eyes on her.

"I wasn't going to... I would've been all right, Mariah."

She swallowed. She reached for the mug and lifted it, pressing the heat of it against her lips. Her throat felt tight. "I know."

"You could've—" He broke off. She heard him crack his knuckles. "You gotta take it easy, Mariah. Take care of yourself." There was an odd note of urgency in his voice.

She felt an ache behind her eyes. She nodded, sipped the milk. "Yes."

He kept standing there. Finally he said, "Okay, now?" His voice was soft and just a little rough.

She gave a quick little nod. "Okay."

"That's all right, then. G'night, Mariah." He turned and padded out of the room.

She sat holding the mug for dear life, blinking rapidly, and wishing...always wishing.

Don't, she warned herself.

But it didn't help. She kept right on wishing until she slept.

Rhys decided the next day that Mariah needed an outing.

"You're not having contractions now, are you? Well, then, I think it's time we broadened your horizons."

What he thought was that the house, big as it was, wasn't big enough for both of them. After last night there was too much awareness between them. There were too many unspoken words, too many half-formed thoughts.

And on his part, at least, way too much need and desire.

And the only way he knew to deal with it was to give them some space—to get out of the house. So he settled her in his car and took her for a drive along the coast.

During the summer months, such a drive would have been insane. Then the roads were clogged with summer people down from the city, day-trippers out for a few hours of sand and surf. Now the road was nearly empty. It was one of those bright late autumn days where there were no clouds at all in the sky and a stiff breeze swept the deserted beaches clean. They drove all the way to Montauk because Mariah said she felt fine, the babies were behaving, and she had no contractions at all.

They ate lunch at a small place near the beach. Then they walked around a little and peered in the windows of shops. One of them, a toy shop, had a window full of stuffed plush bears in all shapes and sizes. Mariah laughed at one with a belly as big as hers.

"Mama Bear," she said. "I love her. I know just how she feels. And look—" She pointed at a pair of smaller ones wearing identical sailor hats and sitting in a sailboat. "Twins."

There were doctor bears, biker bears and teacher bears. One for almost every occupation or hobby. "There." Mariah touched his arm and pointed.

At the far end of the window, Rhys saw a fireman bear perched on a ladder. He wore yellow rubber boots and had a fire hat and a yellow vinyl slicker.

"Isn't he wonderful?" Mariah asked, smiling up at him with such pure delight that it seemed his heart tripped for just a moment before beating steadily on again.

"Yeah," he agreed hoarsely. Then he took her hand. "Come on. We've got a long drive to get home. And you need to rest."

He worried a little that they'd done too much. But any contractions she had that day were mild and irregular. She dutifully took a nap when they got home, and she didn't try to take over when he made dinner.

He complimented her on her restraint.

"I'm trying to be good," she said with a hint of an impish smile. "So we can do something like that again."

The next day he took her to a nearby harbor. They walked along the docks and looked at the boats, and he told her that sometimes he and Dominic hired a boat there and went fishing.

"Have you ever gone sailing?" she asked him.

"I did when I was a kid. It's great."

"We didn't do a lot of sailing in Kansas," she told him.

He looked at her. "Not a lot, huh?"

She grinned. "We didn't do any."

It was another sunny day, but the wind was gone. The temperatures were mild and there was just a soft breeze.

"You want to go sailing for an hour or so?"

"Could we?" Her entire face lit up.

How could a guy say no to that?

It was the most wonderful experience she could ever remember.

She really didn't believe they would be able to do it. How could Rhys conjure up a sailboat, for heaven's sake?

But he found a place that would rent them what he called "a day sailer" for the afternoon.

And the next thing Mariah knew she was being strapped into a life vest and bundled aboard a launch that took them out to a sailboat tied to a mooring. It took some maneuvering to get her from one to the other, and Rhys muttered a lot, mostly about this probably being a really bad idea. But eventually she was sitting in the cockpit, hanging on as they bobbed up and down, and watching with delight as Rhys unfurled the mainsail.

"Can I help?" she asked.

"Yes," he said. "Sit still and stay out of the way."

She sat very still as he did whatever needed to be done. And then the sails were up and crackling in the wind and, whoosh, they were moving lickety-split across the water.

"Oh!" Mariah's breath seemed to catch in her throat. "Oh, my! This is fantastic!" She beamed at him.

And Rhys, settling in the stern with one hand on the tiller, grinned back at her.

They sailed on a zigzag course across the harbor, and Mariah leaned back and tipped her face to the sun, enjoying its warmth as she enjoyed the feel of the wind in her hair. Rhys seemed to be happy, too. He looked younger, more carefree.

The way he used to look.

"It's so quiet," she said. The only things making noise were the sails and the rigging, and the waves that slapped against the side of the boat. She smiled at him again. "Thank you."

He nodded almost soberly. "My pleasure."

They didn't stay out long. And they never went out of the calm water of the harbor. But it didn't matter. She felt refreshed and renewed by the time they tied up again and the launch returned to pick them up.

She yawned mightily when they were back in the car and were heading back to the house.

Rhys said, "Wore you out, did we? I'm sorry."

But Mariah shook her head and said sleepily, "I'm not. It was perfect."

Live for now, her mother always told her.

On afternoons like this one, it wasn't hard to do just that.

Izzy and Chloe gave them a shower.

"I can't come into the city," Mariah said when they told her what they intended.

"No problem," Izzy said cheerfully. "We'll come out there."

"Izzy and Chloe are giving us a shower," Mariah told Rhys that night. Izzy had called her right after supper to sort out the particulars.

"A shower?" Rhys looked surprised and not exactly approving.

"It's a tradition," Mariah said. "To celebrate. We are celebrating, Rhys." She said this last firmly, in case he thought they weren't.

He just nodded his head.

She worried a little that he would find some reason not to be there on Saturday afternoon, which was when Izzy and Chloe had decided it would take place. He seemed to pace around irritably the rest of the week. He talked on the phone a couple of times to a man she guessed was probably his boss, and she halfway expected he might find a fire several thousand miles away that needed his attention right now.

But when she said nervously on Friday night, "You're not leaving, are you?" he just looked at her.

"Of course not." As if there could be no question. "I told you, until these babies are born, I'll be here."

There was a finish line, of course. A deadline. *Until the babies were born...*

And then...?

Live for now, she reminded herself.

It was lovely to see all their friends again.

Izzy and Chloe had invited everyone—Sam and Josie Fletcher, Stella, her editor, Lindy and Gert, the assistants in the office, Damon and Kate Alexakis, Mrs. Alvarez, the Gillespies from upstairs, several more colleagues and neighbors, Rhys's brother Dominic, and, of course, Sierra and Kevin.

She was so glad to see Kevin.

He'd called several times but she'd been asleep every time but one. Now when he came in, she stood up and he took her in his arms and gave her a gentle hug. "You look great," he told her with a grin. "Big as a bus and twice as healthy." He touched her cheek. "Seriously, you do look much better. Is everything okay?"

"Yes," she said, smiling. And it wasn't a lie. It was as okay as it was ever going to be.

"And for you?"

Kevin gave her a rueful smile. "On my own again."

Her own smile slipped and she put a hand on his arm. "There will be someone, Kev."

"Mariah," Rhys said, coming up behind her and taking her arm to steer her away. "Izzy wants your opinion on something."

He had her halfway across the room before she realized it. She looked back and waggled her fingers at Kevin. "Later," she mouthed.

But there was no time later. There was always something happening. Gifts to be opened. Silly games to be played. Cake and ice cream to be served.

It was, as she had said, a celebration.

She opened the gaily wrapped packages and oohed and aahed over the tiny garments and practical diapers and blankets and the double stroller and twin high chairs. She opened them all because Rhys shook his head when Izzy tried to get him to help.

"Let Mariah," he said. And he stood back, leaning against a wall, with his hands in his pockets, and watched.

She was surprised to find one package to her from him. She looked at him curiously. Then she opened it up. Inside was the very pregnant mother bear from the shop in Montauk.

"To keep you company," she read on the card. Her gaze lifted and met his again. His dark eyes were unreadable.

She hugged the bear against her breasts. "Oh, Rhys. Thank you." Their gazes were still locked.

"What are you having? Boys or girls or one of each?" Kate Alexakis asked, and broke the spell.

Mariah shook her head, trying to get back into the moment. "I don't know." The doctor did. He'd offered to tell her, but she'd declined.

"Got names picked out?" Chloe wanted to know.

Mariah looked at Rhys. He looked just as interested as everyone else, and she shook her head again. It wasn't a decision she wanted to make on her own. They were his children, too.

"Better start thinking about it," Finn said. "We're already using up all the good names—Tansy, Pansy, Rip, Crash." He grinned.

"We'll figure it out," Mariah said with one more look at Rhys. She saw Dominic look at him, too, as if assessing his brother's attitude. She wished she could get Dominic alone and talk to him, maybe learn a little more, try to understand.

Everyone stayed after to cook out on the terrace. The day was overcast and everyone but those manning the grills stayed inside. But it was a lively afternoon and evening. Even the babies were up for it—bumping and bouncing against her belly. Mariah winced a time or two after dinner, and Rhys left a conversation he was having with Finn and came across the room to hunker down next to her chair.

"Are you okay?"

"Of course. I'm fine." But a foot against her rib at the very moment she spoke made her grimace again, and she felt a cramping sensation. "It's nothing," she said.

But Rhys wasn't convinced. "You need to lie down."

"I can't lie down! We're in the middle of a party."

"Well, that's easily taken care of." He stood up. "Hey, everybody. Time to go home."

"Rhys!"

But Rhys was adamant. "Mariah needs to rest. Say good-bye, Mariah." He took her hand and began to haul her to her feet.

"Rhys! You don't have to—" she began.

But already Izzy and Finn and Chloe and Gib were gathering things up. Everyone else left, too.

Sierra was the last one out the door. She gave Mariah a hug. "You okay?"

"I'm fine. Truly."

"Good. Rhys is doing a good job."

"Rhys is a bully."

Sierra shrugged. "Just doing what he's supposed to do." She shot him a look that was almost fond. "He's coming around, Mariah."

Mariah glanced quickly in Rhys's direction. He was helping load the presents in Finn's car so they could take them back and put them in her apartment.

"Do you think so?" she asked. She wanted to believe it. Dear God, she wanted to believe it.

"He wouldn't be acting like a guard dog, otherwise," Sierra said. "Once he sees those babies…"

Rhys banged the back of Finn's car down and came over to take Mariah's arm again. "Goodnight, Sierra." It was an order, not a remark.

Sierra grinned and sketched him a salute. Then she looked at Mariah. "What'd I tell you?" she said.

He bossed her along to bed, told her he'd do the cleaning up, and told her he'd be along to check on her shortly.

She hated to admit it—and wouldn't to anyone but herself—but she was beat, and she waddled off to the bedroom without a protest. The kickboxers were going at it with a vengeance tonight, pummeling her and, she imagined, each other.

"You're going to be black and blue when you're born," she told them, twisting and arching her back, trying to give them a few square centimeters more room.

She was in bed when Rhys stuck his head in the door. "Okay?" he asked.

She nodded. "Yes. Thanks. Rhys," she said as he started to back out, "could you do me a favor? Bring me my bear."

He looked startled for just a moment, then nodded and went to fetch it. When he brought the bear back, Mariah cuddled her in her arms and looked up at him. "Thank you again."

He didn't say anything, just stood there. Then he nodded his head.

"It was a nice shower, don't you think?"

Another nod.

She rubbed her cheek against the bear's soft fur. "Could you...um...give me a back rub?"

He swallowed. "If you want."

"Please."

He ran his tongue over his lips. His eyes flickered shut, then opened again. "Let me lock up. I'll be right back."

She was ready when he returned. He flicked off the light and settled onto the bed beside her. She felt his fingers on her back, felt his thumbs press into her spine, felt her own body soften and relax into the rhythm he created.

"Rhys?" Her voice was a whisper almost next to his ear.

He jerked awake, disorientated. Then realized he must have fallen asleep next to her, holding her. He was still on her bed. It was the middle of the night.

He hauled himself up hastily. "S-sorry." He raked a hand through his hair. "D'you need something? Are you okay?"

"I'm fine." He heard her swallow. "But…I think this is it." She gave a nervous little half laugh. "I've been counting for the last hour. The contractions are steady and regular. I think I'm really having the babies."

CHAPTER TEN

THEY weren't going to let him go in with her.

He hadn't taken the prenatal class, they said. He didn't know about breathing and panting and how to coach a woman in childbirth.

"I'm an EMT, damn it. A fireman. I can figure out what to do."

"But she already has a coach," the receptionist, bravest of the lot, said, consulting the paperwork.

"Who?" he demanded and wondered what he'd do if it was Kevin.

"Sierra," Mariah said quietly from the wheelchair beside him. She was very pale now and her breathing seemed shallow. But her grip on his hand was formidable, had been for most of the hour-long trip into the city. He squeezed hers equally hard, then looked down at their entwined fingers, then at her.

"Do you want Sierra?" he asked.

She looked up at him, straight into his eyes and shook her head.

"I want you."

I want you.

It should have sent him running in the other direction.

It made him knuckle down and settle in. It tapped into the best of him—the part that handled crises. He was good in the moment, could handle the demands.

He could handle this.

It was intense. It was demanding. It was the most awe-inspiring experience of his life.

Mariah was the most awe-inspiring person in his life.

He'd always admired her warmth, her openness, her enthusiasm. Since he'd known her he'd considered her mellow and sunny and happy. They'd had good times together.

She was a rock now. Solid to the core.

She was strong and stubborn. Deep and determined.

The doctor told her that the babies were early, that they were small, that they needed every chance.

"The less anaesthetic the better," he told her. "We don't want to dull their responses, slow their hearts."

Mariah listened. She nodded. She clung to Rhys's hand.

"I can give you something if you really need it," the doctor told her. "I'd rather not."

"I can handle it," she assured him. Then she looked at Rhys. "Talk to me."

He talked. They both talked—about everything. About her farm childhood in Kansas, about his New York City youth, about the pranks he and his brothers played and the trouble she and Sierra got into. He could see when the contractions overtook her. He rubbed her back. He fed her ice chips. He massaged her feet.

The contractions grew closer and stronger. Her body trembled and it shuddered. She breathed deep and clutched his hands. They stared into each other's eyes, matching breath for breath.

He never saw her break. She dug deep for inner resources, and came back through each contraction with enough to weather the pain.

Through it all—minutes that seemed hours—hours that went on and on—Mariah was so focused, so determined, so strong.

His function, once she was fairly far along was that of cheerleader and pace-setter. He sat at the head of the birthing bed, his hands locked with hers. They breathed together, they counted together.

"Good job," he told her. "Good going." He felt like a charlatan, giving a pep talk when she had to do all the work. But when he didn't speak she exhorted him to.

"Talk to me, damn it. God! Oh, God!" she exclaimed as another contraction shuddered through her. Then, "I'm…sorry. I'm…breaking your fingers," she gasped when yet another had passed.

Rhys didn't care. He didn't notice. "Go ahead," he said.

"I've got to push," she said frantically.

"Pant," he told her. He didn't know how he knew. He just did. He yelled for the nurse. "Something's happening. Do something!"

"Pant," Mariah whispered to him. There was just a flicker of humor in her eyes.

They clutched hands. The nurse checked her again. "Well, now, yes. Moving right along." She called the doctor. "Come on in."

"Finally," Rhys said. "We're getting somewhere."

But if he thought all the stuff she'd already endured was rough, this was worse. And it was agony for him watching her effort, watching her strain, knowing there was nothing he could do.

"Push," the doctor encouraged her as Rhys mopped her forehead with one hand, the other locked in the death grip of hers. "Yes. Like that. Good. Now hold it. Wait. Wait…. Until you feel it start again. Work with it, Mariah. Okay. Once more. Harder. Harder. That's it." His voice was getting higher. "Yes! Bear down, Mariah!"

She bore. Her face was scarlet, her body shaking. She bit down on her lip. She crushed his fingers in hers. Her gaze flicked up to his.

"S-sorry," she muttered.

"Shh," he said. "I'm the one who's sorry. Sorry I got you into this."

"Don't," Mariah said through clenched teeth. "Don't. Ever. Say. That."

"Yes!" the doctor exclaimed, reaching now and drawing a wriggling, squirming infant into the world. "It's a girl!" he told her.

Mariah laughed and cried at the same time. "Is she…is she…all right?" she asked, watching as the nurses bustled around the whimpering infant.

"All her fingers and all her toes," the doctor said. "Breathing just fine. Dr. Oates will check her over. She's a beauty. See?" He took her from the nurse and held her so Mariah could see her. "See, Dad?"

And there she was, right in front of his eyes. This tiny person. Wiggling. Eyes open as if she were looking for someone.

Rhys nodded numbly, unable to speak.

The doctor handed the baby to the pediatrician who'd just come in. "But we're only half there, aren't we? Still got some work to do. You're doing fine, Mariah. Are you ready?"

Rhys felt her fingers tighten on his once more. She smiled a watery smile at the doctor. "Ready," she said, "whenever you are."

Where she found the strength to do it all again, Rhys didn't know.

But she did—and minutes later a second wriggling dark-haired infant kicked his way into the world.

"Congratulations," the doctor said as he laid this one on Mariah's belly. "You have a daughter and a son."

Rhys looked, but barely saw. His gaze was focused on Mariah.

Her lashes were fluttering. Her fingers shook. Her whole body seemed still to be trembling from equal parts exertion and exhaustion.

"Are you all right?" Rhys demanded.

She smiled at him; tears leaked from the corners of her eyes. "I'm fine," she whispered. She squeezed his hands lightly, as if she had no strength left, which was probably the absolute truth.

"How about you go take a look at your new children," the doctor said briskly to Rhys, "and let us finish up with Mariah here?"

And because she loosed her grip on his hands he moved. Like a sleepwalker, not really taking it all in. He watched with a kind of detached amazement as the pediatrician checked over first one baby, then the other. He watched as the nurses cleaned them and dressed them and wrapped them in tiny blankets, one pink, one blue.

They cried. They flailed their tiny arms and the boy gnawed on his little fist. He kicked his blanket when the nurse wrapped it around him.

Was he the kickboxer? Rhys wondered. Or was it the girl?

Out of the corner of his eye he could see the doctor working over Mariah. She lay so still now. She was so quiet.

"Mr. Kelly?" It was the pediatrician.

Rhys blinked, then realized the man was talking to him. "Wolfe," he said. "My name's Wolfe."

"Oh, right. Sorry. We just had your wife's name. We'll be putting your daughter and son in isolettes for the first twenty-four hours. Just a precaution," he said with a smile, "since they arrived a little early. They seem very healthy, actually. Small, but strong. The boy is five pounds even, the girl, four pounds eleven ounces. Come along with us, and we'll take down the basic family information."

He gave it all by rote. He did whatever they asked him. He didn't think. He sat there in the office and answered questions, vaguely aware of nurses fussing over the babies. Mostly he just played over everything in his head—saw

Mariah working, pushing, panting, straining. Saw it all in his mind's eye all over again.

Where was she?

They'd whisked him out before the doctor had even finished with her. Was she all right? He needed to know she was all right!

"Where's my...where's my wife? I need to see...see my wife." Everyone else was calling her that. Why shouldn't he?

"Just one more section, Mr. Wolfe," the clerk said. "Four more questions."

"Room 411," the nurse told him a minute later, when he came out the door. "She's been asking for you."

He strode quickly down the hall.

She was in bed, her eyes closed, no color at all in her cheeks. He moved closer, desperate to be sure she was breathing. He stumbled over the edge of the bedside table.

Mariah opened her eyes. They were a little bloodshot, but bright.

"Hi." Her voice sounded rusty as if she'd worn it out along with everything else.

"Hey." He edged closer, brushed a strand of hair away from her face, studied it and found a beauty and power in it now that he'd never seen before.

"You were amazing," he told her.

Mariah smiled and put out a hand to touch him and, instinctively, he wrapped his fingers around it. She wasn't trembling now. Her skin felt soft and just a little too cool. He chafed it lightly between his fingers.

"They're amazing," she said softly. "The babies. Thank you, Rhys."

He stared at her, uncomprehending.

Mariah lifted his hand and pressed her lips against it one last time, then did the hardest thing she'd ever done.

"Thank you," she said again. "For the babies. For everything. You don't have to stay, Rhys. You can go."

He went.

Damn right, he went.

It was what he wanted, after all. To be on his own. Free. Unencumbered. To write a check but not to care.

He didn't want to care. Wasn't that what he'd said?

He went away. Went back to Long Island and grabbed his stuff. Went into the city and called his boss.

"I'm ready to go," he said. "Wherever."

"Indonesia," his boss said happily. "Can you catch the next plane?"

He could. He did.

He stopped just briefly at the hospital. He took one last look at those tiny babies. He noticed they had names now. Stephen and Elizabeth.

Good names, he thought. Solid names.

He would have told Mariah so when he stopped to give her the gift he'd brought, but when he glanced in her room she had company. Finn and Izzy were there. And her boss, Stella. And Sierra. And Kevin.

He left the gift at the nurses' station. "See that she gets it," he told them. "I'm in a hurry."

She had all the support she needed.

She didn't need him.

He needed her, though.

He needed *them*. All of them.

Mariah. Elizabeth. Stephen.

A day didn't go by that he didn't think of them. A day? Hell, an hour. Less than an hour. He couldn't get them out of his mind.

He tried to hang onto Sarah and that other baby. Tried

to use them as a shield. But it didn't work. There were no shields for the heart.

Mariah and Stephen and Elizabeth—right along with Sarah and their baby—were on the inside.

His insides.

He fought the fire in Indonesia. He fought the feelings in his heart.

But while the fire died the feelings lived.

He loved them.

He wanted to go home to them.

He wanted to call and talk to Mariah, wanted to find out how she was feeling, if she was coping, if she needed anything. If she needed him.

He was afraid she didn't.

She was so strong, so capable, so competent. She'd clung to his hands during her labor, but she'd done all the work. She'd kissed his fingers when it was done. She'd thanked him for being there, for their children, for everything.

But then she'd let him go.

"Damn it, Mariah." He muttered the words into his pillow a hundred times a night. *Do you love me? Could you ever love me?*

But he couldn't call and ask her that.

He had to see her. Had to look into her eyes. If he could see her eyes when he asked, it wouldn't matter what she said.

If he could see her eyes, he would know.

Kansas at Christmas was a far cry from New York.

No bustling crowds, no lavish window displays, no giant tree in Rockefeller Center.

Well, Mariah supposed the tree was there, but she wasn't. She'd come home for Christmas. She and Sierra had come, bringing Elizabeth and Stephen. Sierra had come for a week.

Mariah and the children had come to stay.

"For a month, three. As long as you want," her parents said. They'd welcomed her—and their two beautiful grand-children—with eager open arms.

And Mariah loved them for it. Loved them for their care, their support, their willingness to take on the burden of helping with middle-of-the-night feedings and colicky ba-bies and her own insecurities.

"I'll get better. I am getting better," she told her mother. She'd been home a week. She'd got a routine. She was even finding a little time to work—an hour here, fifteen minutes there.

"You're doing fine," her mother said. "It takes a lot of people to raise a baby—and you've got two on your own."

She wasn't censorious. She was maybe a little sad. She didn't ask many questions, only if Mariah had loved him.

Mariah had. Mariah still did. She pined for him. She dreamed of him. She rocked her babies and talked to them about him.

"Your daddy is a good man," she told them. "A strong man. A brave man. Someday…someday maybe you'll know…"

His brother Dominic had come by the apartment before she'd left. He'd come bearing gifts—stuffed animals, a cer-tificate for a year's worth of diaper service. She'd let him hold Stephen who'd cried and peed on him.

Dominic had taken it like a man—he'd palmed the baby off on Sierra.

After he left, Mariah had become weepy. Dominic looked so much like Rhys. She said so to Sierra.

Sierra had grunted. "Acts like him, too. Losers, both of them."

"No," Mariah said. Rhys was just a man who knew his limitations.

She knew he'd gone back overseas. She didn't know

where. She never knew where, though she supposed maybe she ought to try to find out—in case...

He might have told her if she'd seen him before he left. She hadn't. She hadn't even known he'd come by when she was still in the hospital until later that afternoon when one of the nurses came in with a box in her hand.

"For you," she'd said. "Your husband left it."

"My—?" Mariah swallowed the last word. Wordlessly she took the box. It was wrapped in pastel gift paper and the card just said, "Twins," and was signed in stark bold script, "Rhys."

She opened it and found the two small bears in the sailboat. She blinked. She swallowed. The tears fell down her cheeks.

The twin bears sat on the nightstand in the twins' bedroom now. Behind them, watching over them, was their very pregnant mom. Mariah rubbed her furry belly every time she passed by.

She did so now on her way to pick up a whimpering Elizabeth. If she could get Lizzie fed before Stephen woke up, she wouldn't have to ask her mother to bottle-feed. She was trying to nurse both of them. It was next to impossible if they were both hungry at the same time.

"Shh, shh, little lady," she crooned now to her fussing daughter. "It's okay. Just a sec." She fumbled with her shirt and the nursing bra. She was much better at it now than she'd been at first.

"I am getting better," she said to herself just as she'd said to her mother. It was becoming a mantra.

Someday she would be able to cope on her own, she was sure of it. Someday life would be fine with just the three of them.

She settled into the rocking chair and cradled Elizabeth against her breast. The baby looked up at her, eyes focusing well now, and glommed on.

Mariah stroked her soft hair, dark hair. Darker than hers. Hair like Rhys's.

She heard the doorbell and ignored it. Her dad had gone out with Sierra to cut the Christmas tree. But her mother was in the kitchen. She would answer. Everyone in Emporia who knew the Kellys had stopped by to see Mariah and her beautiful new twins.

Mariah didn't mind showing them off. She was grateful for the concern and the interest. She was glad she'd come home. She tried to imagine who it would be this time, who hadn't come by yet.

The door opened slightly and her mother stuck her head in. "You've got a visitor."

"Who is it?" There were people Mariah would let in the bedroom to peek at the babies. There were others she'd ask to come back when the twins were awake.

The door opened wider.

"Me." It was Rhys.

Mariah felt her heart soar up to her throat, plummet down to her stomach, then resume beating—about a hundred times faster than it had been—somewhere in between.

She stared at him, disbelieving. Astonished. *Rhys? Here?* "But—"

Behind Rhys, Mariah saw her mother smile at her, then step back and shut the door.

He looked wonderful. Tanned and strong and handsome as the devil. He wore faded jeans and a sweater and there were snowflakes still clinging to his hair.

"Rhys!" She smiled. But she didn't go to him. Couldn't, of course, because she was nursing the baby. But she didn't think she could have anyway. If she had, she might have clung, have grabbed on and held him. She'd been strong once.

But once might have been her limit.

She couldn't do it again. Not and let him go.

"What a…surprise." She tried to sound cheerful. She just sounded nervous. She wetted suddenly dry lips. "Why are you—?" No, she couldn't ask that. "How nice you came for Christmas."

There, that was better. Polite. Distant. Noncommittal.

"I didn't come for Christmas," he said. His voice was rough, and as nervous as hers, she thought with surprise.

Her eyes widened. She saw him swallow, saw his knuckles whiten against the Christmas present he clutched in his hands.

Why, then…? she started to ask.

But before she could he answered. "I came because I love you."

She went perfectly still. She stared at him, looked into his eyes—unhappy eyes, she thought. Anguished eyes. Desperate eyes.

Desperate for her?

It didn't seem possible.

And yet…

His fingers were crushing the box. His eyes were boring into hers. "I know you don't need me, Mariah. I know I didn't want you to. I can't expect you to love me, but—"

"I do."

The sound of Christmas, Mariah always thought, was silence. It was expectation. It was hope. It was possibility, however unexpected.

It was Rhys's sharply indrawn breath.

And then he crossed the room in three quick strides and knelt beside her. He wrapped his arms around her, around Elizabeth. He pressed his face into the curve of her neck, and he wept.

Mariah wept, too. She dripped salty tears on Elizabeth's cheek. She rubbed more against Rhys's soft hair. She said, "I love you. I love you. I love you," over and over and over.

And he said the same to her.

When he drew back at last, they looked at each other and smiled, then they laughed a little. Then he wiped the tears off her face and she did the same to his. Then he looked down at Elizabeth who had nursed through the whole event with supreme indifference and now regarded her father curiously.

"She's huge," he said, awe in his voice.

"Almost six pounds," Mariah said.

Across the room, Stephen began fussing. Mariah shifted Elizabeth to her shoulder to burp her. "Could you bring me Stephen?"

For a moment Rhys didn't move. Then he nodded. He went to the crib and carefully, gingerly almost, lifted out his son. Holding him with awkward tenderness, he brought the baby to his mother.

"How can you—?" He nodded at Elizabeth, then at Stephen, clearly wondering how Mariah was going to handle both.

She wasn't. "Trade you," she said and deftly handed him his daughter.

For a second he bobbled her, then clasped her firmly against his chest.

"Pat her back," Mariah said. "She needs to burp. Here. Put this diaper on your shoulder."

One-handed, Rhys arranged the diaper. And as Stephen began to nurse Rhys patted his daughter's back and was rewarded with a tiny belch.

He grinned. He laughed. "I did it!"

Mariah laughed, too, though a few more tears leaked out as well. "You did."

He walked around the room, still patting Elizabeth while Mariah nursed Stephen. They were a team.

Moments later her mother stuck her head in again and smiled at what she saw. "Exactly the way it should be," she said and went off to tell her husband and Sierra the good news.

She showed Rhys how to change the babies. He didn't think they were so big then. His fingers seemed all thumbs as he tried to get the diapers on.

"You'll get the hang of it," she promised him. "I did."

"I will," Rhys vowed.

They stood there together, watching their children, and Mariah felt Rhys's fingers wrap around hers. They clung.

"What's in the package?" she asked him.

He picked it up from where he'd set it on the floor and handed it to her. "Open it."

"I don't have to wait for Christmas?"

"I hope you won't."

She opened it with nerveless fingers, tore off the wrapping, took off the lid.

It was the fireman bear. With his hat and his boots and his yellow slicker. There was a tiny paper folded in the pocket of his slicker. Mariah pulled it out.

There was a ring attached. *Will you marry me?* it said.

She turned to Rhys and handed him the ring.

He looked first at it, then, desperately, at her.

She held out her hand and gave him her love in her eyes. "Will you put it on?"

He did.

The first time they'd made love, it had been a love born of pain. It had been beautiful and life-giving in more ways than one. It had redeemed him even though he hadn't known it at the time.

This time, Rhys vowed, was for her.

This time he would love her with joy and with passion, with care and consideration. He would show her with his body how deeply he loved her.

When the doctor said it was all right—and the babies

were eight weeks, not six—he got his parents-in-law to watch their grandchildren for the night, and he spirited Mariah away.

"Where are we going?" she asked. "What are you up to?"

He just grinned. He'd made plans. Done research. Found a hideaway.

It was in the middle of nowhere. A cabin on a farm. Rustic and out of the way, but perfect for a couple who had no need of anyone or anything but each other.

"Trust me," he said, folding her hands in his.

She did.

It looked a little more rustic now than when he'd come here to check it out. The wind was whipping across the hills, the first snowflakes stung. He wondered if maybe this was a good idea.

"I love it," Mariah said. She put her arms around him. She kissed his cheek. He shifted so she kissed his lips. And he kissed hers. It was a hungry, desperate kiss.

"You build a fire," Mariah said. "I'll make the bed."

"Bed's made," Rhys told her. He'd been there this morning, had brought the champagne glasses and the meal he intended to cook for her. But now that they were here he wasn't hungry.

"Are you hungry?" he asked her.

She laid her hands on his chest. "For you," she said.

They barely made it to the bed.

So much for care and consideration. So much for finesse. But at least there was passion. He had that. And intensity. God, yes.

Their clothes lay where they fell. He would build the fire later. There was already a fire burning hot and deep within both of them.

They burrowed under the down quilt and learned each other's body. His rough and hers smooth. His hard and hers soft. He kissed her lips, her throat, her breasts. With his hands he learned the curves and slopes and valleys of her body. He remembered it slim and pliant, he remembered it full, burgeoning with their children. He found it now, full and soft and yielding. Damp. Ready.

For him.

She drew him in. She wrapped him in her warmth, in her sweetness, in her love.

She kissed him, loved him, shattered him.

And made him whole again.

They built the fire later. Much later.

They cooked the meal and drank the champagne. Then they wrapped themselves in the quilt once more and Mariah nestled against the heart of the man she loved.

She traced a circle on his chest and made him shiver. She ran her foot up his calf and touched the inside of his thigh. He let out a soft, low growling sound.

"You're asking for trouble," he told her and nipped her ear.

"Am I?" She was delighted. Her foot inched farther. Her hands did wicked teasing things. He shifted. He moaned.

"Mmm," he murmured, capturing her hands, "and you're finding it, too."

And he rolled her onto her back and plunged in. He was hard and she was slick, and it was marvelous. Quick. Fierce. Quenching.

And after, sated, she wrapped her arms around him. "You were wonderful," she told him. "You are wonderful. You put my fire right out."

Rhys lifted himself far enough to look down at her with those beautiful midnight eyes.

"I hope not," he said gruffly, and he lowered his head and kissed her long and hard and deep. "I hope not. I don't want this fire to go out. Ever."